Cowboy at Heart

SHIPMENT FIVE

Belonging to Bandera by Tina Leonard
Court Me, Cowboy by Barbara White Daille
His Best Friend's Bride by Jodi O'Donnell
The Cowboy's Return by Linda Warren
Baby Be Mine by Victoria Pade
The Cattle Baron by Margaret Way

SHIPMENT SIX

Crockett's Seduction by Tina Leonard
Coming Home to the Cattleman by Judy Christenberry
Almost Perfect by Judy Duarte
Cowboy Dad by Cathy McDavid
Real Cowboys by Roz Denny Fox
The Rancher Wore Suits by Rita Herron
Falling for the Texas Tycoon by Karen Rose Smith

SHIPMENT SEVEN

Last's Temptation by Tina Leonard
Daddy by Choice by Marin Thomas
The Cowboy, the Baby and the Bride-to-Be by Cara Colter
Luke's Proposal by Lois Faye Dyer
The Truth About Cowboys by Margot Early
The Other Side of Paradise by Laurie Paige

SHIPMENT EIGHT

Mason's Marriage by Tina Leonard
Bride at Briar's Ridge by Margaret Way
Texas Bluff by Linda Warren
Cupid and the Cowboy by Carol Finch
The Horseman's Son by Delores Fossen
Cattleman's Bride-to-Be by Lois Faye Dyer

**The rugged, masculine and independent men
of America's West know the value of hard work,
honor and family. They may be ranchers, tycoons
or the guy next door, but they are all cowboys at heart.
Don't miss any of the books in this collection!**

Cowboy at Heart

THE OTHER SIDE OF PARADISE

LAURIE PAIGE

USA TODAY Bestselling Author

HARLEQUIN® COWBOY AT HEART

Recycling programs
for this product may
not exist in your area.

ISBN-13: 978-0-373-82645-2

THE OTHER SIDE OF PARADISE

Copyright © 2005 by Olivia M. Hall

Printed in U.S.A.

LAURIE PAIGE

"One of the nicest things about writing romances is researching locales, careers and ideas. In the interest of authenticity, most writers will try anything…once." Along with her writing adventures, Laurie has been a NASA engineer, a past president of the Romance Writers of America, and is a mother and a grandmother. She was twice a Romance Writers of America RITA® Award finalist for Best Traditional Romance and has won awards from *RT Book Reviews* for Best Silhouette Special Edition and Best Silhouette, in addition to appearing on the *USA TODAY* bestseller list.

Chapter One

Mary McHale checked the directions on the sheet of paper, then studied the road again. There was no indication of a one-lane bridge on the quickly sketched map at the bottom of the brochure, nor of a creek.

Before retracing her tracks to the main county road, she perused the evergreen forest rising up the steep slope of the mountain, listened to the sound of the quietly burbling creek under the wooden bridge, then wondered if the water was pure enough to drink.

Not that she would risk taking a sip, but the woodland scene looked so peaceful and inviting it was difficult to imagine danger lurking there, whether germs or other kinds.

A place to lose yourself. Or maybe, she mused, a place to lose the world and find yourself.

The deep quiet called to her, but she had obligations and, as some poet had once said, miles to go before she slept.

With a sigh, she wheeled the old SUV and horse trailer in a tight arc and started back the way she'd come. At the main county road, she headed north once more and continued her search for the Towbridge ranch.

Three miles farther on, another gravel lane forked to the left. She spotted the sign informing her that the place she sought was seven miles west and made the correct turn.

Relief wafted through her. The shadows were long, she was tired and Attila needed food, water and exercise.

Nearly twenty minutes and seven miles later, she pulled up before the main building, a timber structure built rather like a large hunting lodge. A sign over the front porch declared the place to be the Towbridge Ranch, Est. 1899.

The gravel driveway continued on and circled a wooded area dotted with three or four picnic tables. Around the western perimeter of the driveway, she spotted campsites through the firs and pine trees. RVs filled most of the parking spaces.

Well, it was the first Monday of September. Labor Day. Families were enjoying their last weekend in the mountains before winter set in, she supposed.

After parking before an old-fashioned horse rail, obviously new, she picked up a postcard from the passenger seat. It showed the seven peaks that formed a semicircle along the eastern border of Hells Canyon and gave the area its name. Seven Devils Mountains.

The peaks were west of the camp-ranch-resort where she was to be employed as a wrangler-hiking-guide-whatever. The sun was setting behind the mountains in a near replica of the scene on the postcard she'd impulsively bought in Lost Valley, Idaho, the small town where she'd gassed up and which was an hour's drive down the winding, dusty mountain roads she'd just traveled.

Observing the pink, gold and magenta streaks of the sunset and the mysterious shadows of the forest, she experienced the oddest sensation—that of a weight settling on her spirit. A forlorn sadness accompanied the heaviness, as if something vast and terrible impinged on her soul…a tragedy…

The emotion puzzled and irritated her. Seven Devils. The name was almost a premonition, a black cloud lurking on the horizon. Maybe she'd been here in a past life.

Yeah, right, and maybe she'd been Cleopatra in another.

A soft neigh from Attila, reminding her of his needs, pulled her out of the introspective mood. She had things to do and people to see.

After backing the horse out of the trailer, she snapped a lead rope on his halter and tied it at the end of the railing so he could munch the fall grass while she went inside to report to her new bosses, Keith Towbridge and Jonah Lanigan.

The lodge was empty. She surveyed the quaint main room, which had a high ceiling, a huge fireplace and rustic furniture made from alder and white cedar.

To her left was an office with a counter separating it from the great room. An archway to the right disclosed a small store stocked with canned goods and camping gear. A staircase gave access to rooms on the second floor while a hallway led to the nether regions on the main level of the sturdy building.

According to the brochure she'd picked up in town, the place was advertised as an adventure destination in the real West, which apparently meant hunting, fishing and paramilitary games for those "wanting to break out of the ordinary routine of life." That idea would appeal to the deskbound executive, she supposed.

"Anybody here?" she called.

The place was so silent she could hear grass grow if she listened hard enough. The hair on her nape stood up.

"Hello!" she yelled more forcibly.

"Hello, yourself," a masculine voice finally replied. "I'm in the kitchen."

She walked down the hall and into a galley-type kitchen. Directly across from it was a room with three tables, each with four chairs. Windows displayed the view in three directions—all magnificent.

A man, as long-legged and lean as a coyote, glanced at her while he continued a chore at the sink. His features were hawkish, the angles of his face stern but attractive in a hard-jawed, clean-shaven way.

Like her, he was dressed in boots, jeans and a white T-shirt. He also wore a blue work shirt, open down the front, over the tee. Unlike her, he wore no hat. She liked to keep her hair tucked out of sight under a worn gray Stetson.

"You the new wrangler?" he asked.

"Yes."

"Who sent you here?"

She wondered if this was a trick question. "Trek Lanigan from the Trading Post north of Lost Valley. Are you his cousin?"

The Trading Post was a store that sold Native American crafts some of it old and valuable. That was where she'd seen the Help Wanted sign and asked about the job. The owner of the store bore a distinct resemblance to this man, except he wore his hair long. This one kept his cut short.

Glancing at the dining room, she realized she'd expected more of a working ranch and less of a resort type place. She didn't like being around people all the time.

Most of the time, she amended.

The man nodded, affirming he was the cousin who'd hired her by phone interview. He finished washing a potato and dropped it in a pot of what looked like simmering soup stock. The pot was huge, the aroma coming from it mouthwatering.

"Can you cook?" he wanted to know.

"Yes. But Mr. Lanigan didn't mention it as a requirement."

"He's Trek. I'm Jonah. Keith Towbridge is my partner. His wife is Janis. They have a son, K.J., short for Keith, Junior. Their house is on the back of the ranch, but they're over here fairly often. You'll meet them later this week."

Mary took in the information and stored it for future reference. It sounded as if she had definitely been hired. For now. At least he hadn't taken one look and told her to get lost. The owners could probably use all the help they could get out here in the wilds.

"I, uh, have to take care of my horse. He needs water and bedding down."

Jonah Lanigan shot her another assessing glance. His hair was almost black, his eyes a smoky blue-gray that effectively hid his thoughts. He was four or five inches taller than her own five feet ten inches.

In her work boots, she was as tall or taller than most men. Her height usually gave her an advantage, but not with this man. She stirred uneasily.

"The stable is in back." He frowned and she noted the irritation he suppressed. "There's a bunkhouse attached. I suppose we can make room in the lodge, though."

"The bunkhouse is fine," she quickly told him. "Uh, if I have a private bedroom?"

He shook his head. "There's an empty room at the top of the stairs. Put your stuff up there for now. I'll need your help at breakfast. Six o'clock sharp."

"Right." She retreated.

So far, so good. She'd made it past the first hurdle. The rancher down in the valley had taken one look at her and said the wrangler job she'd come there to fill wasn't open. His son had looked her over with obvious interest.

She probably had an Equal Opportunity case against the older man, but she hadn't liked his manner—nor his son's—or the poor condition of the ranch and stock, so she'd left without arguing.

Attila whickered as soon as she appeared. She soothed him with a few quiet words, untied the rope, then led the horse around the lodge to the backyard where she spotted the stable. There was a fenced area next to it.

After freeing the nine-year-old stallion in the paddock, she filled a trough with fresh water, then checked the stable.

The eight stalls were empty. She prepared one for her horse, placing hay in the manger and spreading fresh straw over the dirt floor. Finished, she went outside and observed the dun-colored thoroughbred as he walked around the fence and checked out his new quarters.

His silver coat with the brownish tinge— really a dark ash-blond—seemed a lighter shade against the weathered gray of the stable. His limp wasn't pronounced, but she was aware of his fatigue in the way he moved.

A racehorse that hadn't done well at the track, he'd been placed in a stock auction three years ago, but few had wanted the spirited stallion. He was useless as a work horse and parents hadn't thought him safe for their children.

However, his bloodlines were excellent, and Mary had seen promise in the powerful haunches that had lifted him over a seven-foot fence when he'd attempted an escape. Using her life savings of fourteen thousand dollars, she'd outbid the other person who'd been interested in buying him.

Attila was the one thing she loved in all the world. They had bonded the first time she'd petted him at the track where she'd worked as a handler, getting the excited horses in the slots so the races could begin.

Noticing a cabin connected to the stable via an enclosed breezeway, she knocked on the door, then entered when no one answered. The place had a main room with a wood-stove and two smaller rooms behind that. Bedrooms, she discovered upon further exploration. The building hadn't been used in a while, she decided, swiping a finger through the dust on a sturdy pine table in the first room.

The ranch apparently didn't hire many

workers. That was fine by her. Here, she would have privacy.

Pleased, she hurried back to the lodge to move the SUV and trailer down, then decided first she'd better ask her boss about staying in the cabin.

From the kitchen, she heard a string of curses as she mounted the steps to the back entrance. Smoke billowed from the screen door. Her boss came outside just as she approached wearing oven mittens and carrying a baking sheet of black lumps. With a couple of added curses, he tossed lumps, pan and all over the railing and onto the dried lawn.

"That could start a grass fire," she mentioned in carefully casual tones.

He grabbed a hose from a reel mounted on the house and drenched the biscuits or whatever the lumps had been in their former incarnation, then turned off the water with a furious twist. "There, satisfied?" He stomped inside.

She followed, wary of his temper but curious about him and the operations of the resort. "Do you need some help?"

Giving her a look that should have sizzled

her to charcoal, he nodded. "Can you make biscuits?"

After the briefest hesitation, she said she could. Spotting a bag of cornmeal, she added, "How about some cornbread? People like that with soup."

"Whatever."

He clearly wasn't in the mood to discuss it. She washed her hands and set to work. In a few minutes, she slid a skillet of cornbread into the oven. When he left to answer the phone in the office, she quickly tasted the soup.

It was pretty good, but a bit salty. She added some pasta curls to absorb the salt and a dash of pepper to give it a little more balance. She also added garlic powder and a few dried onion flakes, plus a scant tablespoon of sugar.

After retrieving the baking pan from the lawn, she scrubbed it at the stainless steel sink, dried it, then put it with some pie pans she found in a cabinet beside the stove. Spotting a timer, she set it so she'd remember to check the cornbread, then explored the kitchen more fully. If she was also going to be the cook and chief bottle washer—and it looked as if that was her fate—she'd better know her way around.

"Do you serve dinner every night?" she asked when Jonah returned.

"Only when we have guests in the lodge. Right now we have six men here on a business retreat. They've been doing war games all week, but this is their last day. They'll be leaving in the morning. Then we're free until the hunters start coming in next month."

"You don't employ a cook?"

"She quit."

Mary heard the undercurrent of anger in his voice, saw it in the tightening of his jaw. He looked like a man who could bite off iron and spit out horseshoes, as the starter at the race track used to say.

Her new boss continued. "It was too isolated, too lonely out here to spend a winter, she said."

"Did she mean something to you?"

He looked rather startled at the question. "Not personally, if that's what you're thinking. I don't get involved with the hired help."

"Good idea," she said and meant it. She relaxed a bit. She made it a rule not to get involved with anyone, so they were on the same wavelength. "I looked at the bunkhouse. No one seems to be using it."

"That's right. Keith and I have managed to run things without much help in the past, but business has picked up this summer. Companies like to use our place for retreats because it's cheap."

She wasn't interested in the business prospects at the moment. "I can stay out there. That'll keep the room here in the lodge free for paying guests."

He shook his head. "It hasn't been modernized. There's no running water, and the only heat is from the stove."

"I don't mind—"

"I do. It'll be easier all around if you stay in the lodge. Winter can come early here in the mountains. There's no sense in wasting firewood out there."

"You seemed to think it was okay for a male."

"I thought he could cut his own firewood."

"I can do that."

He stuck his hands on his hips and gave

her an impatient glare. "You won't have time. I need help with the paying customers. We make them happy campers, they come back next year or tell their friends about the place. That means money."

She understood the imperatives of finance all too well. "Fine. Uh, where do you and the Towbridges stay?"

"I have a room on the other side of the office. Keith and Janis have the original ranch house over at the other camp, about a mile down the road from here."

Again she stored the info. The lodge and ranch were bigger than she'd first thought. The main structure was new or had been extensively remodeled. The bunkhouse and stable weren't, but both had been repaired recently. The place had an air of...not exactly prosperity, but of hard work and plans for the future.

Up until three months ago, she'd had big plans, too—the Olympics with her and Attila in the cross-country steeplechase. As she'd thought, he was a powerful jumper and had a competitive spirit. He'd just needed careful training and someone he could trust to bring out his talents.

But early in June, leading in an important trial, he'd pulled up lame. A sprained tendon, the vet had said. Rest and several months of mending had been the recommended cure.

She'd needed a job and he'd needed a place to heal. So here they were. Actually this looked like the ideal situation. She would take care of the horses, which were out on the trail, she assumed, and help cook when necessary.

The timer dinged.

After removing the golden-brown cornbread from the oven, she flipped it out onto a platter, turned the oven off, wiped out the skillet and set it on the back of the stove, then glanced around to see what else was to be done.

Jonah was leaning against the doorway, observing her every move. Her insides tightened at the scrutiny, but she didn't let her tension show. Instead she gazed back at him, her expression devoid of any emotion while she wondered what it was about him that made her nervous.

It wasn't simply that he was attractive. He

was that and more, but she'd met other handsome, self-confident men in her work. Perhaps it was the alert intelligence in his eyes. His earlier irritation over the cooking disaster was gone, replaced by curiosity. She liked anger better. It was focused emotion that didn't lead to questions. Curiosity, coupled with a keen mind, often did. She had a gut feeling that he thought a female wrangler might be more trouble than she was worth.

"What's next?" she asked with false cheer.

"You'll have six horses and two pack mules to see to when the men get here. Keith called. They're on their way."

"I'll put fresh straw in the stalls. I noticed the round bales in the lean-to beside the stable. Is that what I should use?"

He nodded.

She left by the back door, glad to escape his perusal. He'd nearly made her stutter with that penetrating stare. From now on, she'd be on guard. She hated showing any signs of weakness to an enemy.

Enemy? Jonah Lanigan was simply a man harried by a shortage of help. He was her boss, nothing more or less. He couldn't hurt her. No one could, unless she left herself open and vulnerable.

Glancing over her shoulder, she stopped abruptly. The far peaks were sharp and black against the twilight sky. They jutted up beyond the surrounding hills like jagged teeth, their silhouettes wicked and threatening. She felt danger all around—

The door banged behind her.

Jonah came out on the porch. "The men are here. Go take care of the animals and their gear. You also need to stop by the office and fill out some forms."

She nodded and went to meet the bearded and unkempt adventurers at the stable. "Hi. I'm Mary, the wrangler," she told them, friendly but casual. "I'll handle the stock. Go on inside. The soup is ready."

"Thank God," one of the weary travelers murmured. "I haven't been so tired since I was nine and our scout troop got lost and marched ten extra miles before finding the place we were to camp."

"Good thing you had some experience in the woods," one of the other men said. "We would still be wandering around in the hills otherwise."

The first man looked pleased. "We did pretty good at getting back by ourselves, didn't we?"

Mary witnessed new energy enter the little group of warriors as they recalled their accomplishments over the long weekend. They'd planned strategy and held mock battles with paint balls. They had worked on their team skills as well as their navigational ones.

"And found our inner man, uh, men, or something like that," a third added, causing the others to chuckle.

"The boss will be proud when we report back." The first man gave Mary a wink and handed over the reins to his mount, a gentle cowpony now gray in the muzzle.

After releasing the horses and pack mules into the paddock, she led each one in turn into the stable. She cleaned their hooves and groomed their coats, then fed and watered them.

She left one mule in the paddock while she reluctantly moved Attila under the lean-to and made him a bed in there, with a pole propped between two bales of straw to keep him enclosed. Tomorrow she could look around and maybe figure out another arrangement.

After caring for the last mule, she drove her vehicles to the rear, retrieved her bags from the SUV, then trudged up the barely discernible path to the lodge. From the dining room came sounds of merriment and lots of teasing about their exploits among the six men. She quietly walked along the corridor to the stairs.

From the office, she could hear the deep voice of her boss. "Yeah, she arrived," he said.

She stopped upon realizing he was discussing her.

"She seems to know her way around. Did you know she has a horse? She does," he said when the other person obviously replied in the negative. "One thing, she can cook. She did something to fix the soup and also made cornbread when I burnt the biscuits. So maybe she won't be a total loss."

Mary's chest lifted in indignation at the implied criticism. She quelled the emotion and the urge to storm in and inform her boss that she was a damn good worker. People new to an area were often viewed with suspicion, and she couldn't afford the luxury of hurt feelings.

"Well," he continued as if explaining his remark, "she's as skinny as a birch twig. The first winter wind might blow her away. I don't know if she has the strength to do the job." He chuckled sardonically. "Yeah, I know, beggars can't be choosers. Thanks a lot, cuz."

Before Mary could move, he hung up and walked into the hallway, now alight with the soft glow of two wall sconces.

Their eyes met.

"Sorry. I didn't know you were out here," he said.

She shrugged. "Lots of men don't think women can do the job. We have to prove ourselves each time. It comes with the territory." She spoke carefully, determined not to let him rattle her.

"You'll have to help me with the hunting parties this fall. We'll be setting up blinds, maybe wading through snow up to our boot tops." There was a warning in his tone.

"I'm not afraid of hard work."

Only of people, but she didn't say that.

She wasn't really afraid of anyone, but she'd learned to be wary.

"Good, 'cause we have plenty of it around here." He started toward the kitchen area.

She went up two steps.

"Your cornbread was a hit with the men," he added.

Glancing over her shoulder, she nodded.

"And the soup. What did you do to it?"

"Added some spices."

His smile was sudden and unexpected. "You'll have to show me what and how much. My attempts at cooking are unreliable, as you observed earlier."

Mary experienced a flutter in the pit of her stomach at the rueful humor evident in his eyes. "Sure," she said and moved up another step.

His next words stopped her cold. "You have a very precise way of speaking," he murmured, looking at her in a quizzical manner as if trying to figure out what made her tick.

She hesitated, not sure how much she wanted to disclose but feeling compelled to tell him some of the truth. "I had speech therapy when I was a kid."

His eyebrows rose slightly. "Yeah? Why was that?"

Every muscle in her body went rigid at the question. She realized she'd set herself up for an inquisition, but it still took a second for her to regain her poise. She gave him a level stare. "When I started kindergarten, I had a stutter. In first grade, I was placed in Special Ed for therapy."

She had to pause in saying the last word to prevent the stutter from returning. She'd learned to slow down, to breathe calmly while she heard the word in her mind, then to say it.

A ripple of emotion went through his eyes. For a second she thought he could see right down into the chasm where her soul dwelt, but he didn't mouth any platitudes and meaningless compassionate phrases. He simply nodded as if her words explained everything and went on his way.

Mary exhaled sharply, then continued up the stairs and into the room he'd said she was to have. She closed and locked the door behind her, then stood there panting as if she'd barely escaped from a trap.

"I'm not afraid of him," she said aloud,

her face in the dresser mirror set and angry. "I'm not a child. I don't ever have to be afraid again."

But the memories flooded into her mind— of times when she'd been terrified, of loneliness so intense she'd felt a part of her innermost self had been ripped away, of helplessness because she was a child and her world was filled with strangers who decided her life without consulting her.

The man who was assumed to be her father had abandoned her at a bar in Wyoming. She'd remembered her nickname and that she was three years old, but she didn't know what had happened to her mother or where their home was. She'd thought she had lots of family at one time, but maybe that was the fantasy of a lonely child.

Two things she remembered very well— the shock of having her head shaved when she was put into the orphanage and the year it had taken for her hair to grow long enough so that her image in a mirror no longer frightened her. For the first four months of that year, she'd quit speaking entirely. She'd felt as if her *real* self had been stolen. She hadn't known who she was, where she belonged.

Sometimes, she mused, she felt as if she still didn't. Perhaps that was why she didn't like to stay in one place too long. She was looking for the little girl who'd been lost all those years ago…

With a confused sigh, she settled on one of the twin beds in the neat room. Since arriving in Lost Valley that afternoon, she'd felt unsettled and anxious.

She didn't know why. It wasn't as if she'd ever been there or had known anyone who'd ever lived in the area.

However, something about the name— Seven Devils—haunted her. While waiting for Jonah's cousin at the Trading Post to sketch the map on the brochure advertising the ranch, she'd read the legend of the seven monsters who'd crossed the river and eaten the children until Coyote had turned them into the seven peaks grouped around the eastern side of the Snake River. For some reason the story had both intrigued and bothered her.

A shiver ran along her spine as apprehension seized her. She felt danger all around, but she didn't know if it came from within herself or the seven devils of the legend.

Or from the tall, handsome man whose keen gaze saw more than she wanted to reveal.

Chapter Two

Jonah spotted the forms on the pass-through counter to the office at once the next morning. Since it was barely daylight, he wondered when his new helper had filled them out. He swiftly read the information.

Mary McHale was twenty-six years old. Her birthday was in March. Her mailing address was in care of general delivery at a post office in Wyoming. She'd apparently grown up on a ranch and had worked with horses at rodeos for six years, moving from place to place, then had worked two years in California at a racetrack. Most of the current year had been spent qualifying her horse in steeplechase trials.

Man, she was dreaming big if she was thinking of making the international circuit, or maybe even the Olympic Games.

He finished reading the info. On the next-of-kin line she'd written "None."

His glance flicked back to the address line. The name of the place was familiar, but from what? Ah, yes. He'd received mailings from there asking for donations for a children's ranch run by some church group a couple of times this past year. An orphan. That's why she had no kin.

An unusual emotion shot through him. It took a minute to recognize it as pity. The loneliness implied by having no relatives pinged through him. He thought of all the real and honorary aunts, uncles and cousins he had on the Indian side of his family, of the noisy Irish clan on the paternal side.

It must be tough to be cut off from your relatives, to have no one at all.

He broke off the pitying thought. Other than her working skills and references, her life wasn't his business.

He'd checked out their animals last night and found them well tended. Okay, so she was experienced as a wrangler. He'd also noticed her horse in a makeshift stall and saw that it had one leg wrapped in elastic bandage. The big stallion had limped when it came over to sniff him.

That explained why she wasn't competing now.

Glancing out the window at her rig, he wondered if she'd pinned all her hopes on the dun-colored jumper.

He could identify with that. He and Keith had sunk all they had into making this old ranch that had belonged to Keith's grandfather into a profitable business once more.

They were actually managing to do that, but only by running an RV camp in the summer and a hunting lodge in the fall and early winter. They also held business retreats and paramilitary games to teach strategy, teamwork and thinking outside the box. He had a reputation as an expert in that department, one that he'd cultivated for business purposes.

With an MBA from Wharton, he'd worked for ten years as an ad executive in New York. During that time, he'd also written a bestselling book on business techniques. When he'd reached the point that he couldn't stand making up another slogan or jingle for a thirty-second sound bite, he'd returned to his roots for a vacation and ended up buying into the ranch with Keith and staying, much to his mother's delight.

He punched the new wrangler's info into the computer and added her to the payroll. He sent an e-mail to their insurance agent to include her on the business account for health as well as workmen's comp.

Keith would question the latter decision, but Jonah figured she couldn't afford it on her own. If she could handle the stock and help at the lodge, they would have to give her a raise, too. That was only fair.

Hearing noise outside, he filed the employment forms and headed for the back. He lifted his head and sniffed the air as he strode along the corridor. A delicious aroma came from the kitchen.

There he found coffee already brewed in the big urn. Fresh muffins were piled in a towel-lined basket. After filling a cup, he grabbed a muffin and bit into the heavenly taste of nuts and blueberries.

Ignoring the chill of early morning in the mountains, he went out on the porch with the food. He saw the trail horses and pack mules were in the correct pasture. The big dun was with them.

He went inside for another muffin and returned to the porch. The hired help was walking up the path.

"Good morning," he said.

Her head jerked up in surprise. Or maybe alarm. It was difficult to tell. As she had yesterday, she wore glasses that went from a light tint to dark gray according to the degree of light. Her hair was tucked under her hat.

This morning she wore a long-sleeved plaid shirt over a blue T-shirt with jeans and boots. Her hands were in her pockets and leather gloves dangled from her waistband.

"Hello," she said, giving out the word cautiously, as if she didn't trust him with more from her.

"These muffins are great," he said. "You must have been up at first light."

She shrugged, checked that her boots were clean and came up the steps to the porch. "I was awake."

He wondered if she'd slept. Not that it was any of his business. "By the way, the mules like to bunk together, so you can put your stallion in the stable."

Pausing on the top step, she considered the words as if for a hidden mine, then nodded. "Thanks." She went inside.

In the kitchen, he finished off the second muffin, then observed while she poured milk and a mug of coffee before turning to him. "Okay if I have eggs for breakfast?"

"Help yourself."

She removed two eggs, then glanced his way. "You want half an omelet?"

"Sounds good."

Looking as serious as a surgeon, she retrieved two more eggs along with butter and cheese. Spotting the left-over ham he'd been using for sandwiches, she cut some of that and soon had the omelet in the skillet.

"You're efficient in the kitchen," he commented, refilling his coffee mug.

Her hesitation was long enough to be noticed. "I went through a work-study program my last year of school and was trained as a short-order cook."

"The orphanage made sure you had a skill before you were sent out on your own, huh?"

She visibly started. "How did you—" She stopped abruptly.

"I recognized the name of the town on the form," he said, keeping his tone neutral. "The church sent me a couple of brochures about the work at the children's ranch. I have no idea how they got my name."

"They buy lists," she said curtly. "Names and addresses. The students type them into a computer file for mailings."

She frowned as if chagrined that she'd disclosed this much, then cut the omelet into two parts and gave him the largest piece along with two slices of buttered toast. When she set her plate at the end of the counter, it was clear she intended to eat standing up.

"Let's go into the dining room while we have it to ourselves," he suggested. "Our guests won't get up for a couple of hours."

He led the way across the hall and took a seat by the window. She put her plate down and returned to the kitchen for her milk and coffee. Jonah removed a fork from a container such as those used for straws at soda fountains.

"That's a good idea," she said, coming back to the table. She selected a fork for herself.

"I thought it was more convenient to have the utensils, on the tables along with salt and pepper shakers, napkins and sugar bowls. People can serve themselves." He took a bite of the omelet. "Mmm, this is good."

"Thanks."

They ate in silence. The former house-keeper and cook, a middle-aged widow, had talked way too much. This woman spoke very little. That fact intrigued him.

"You don't talk much," he said.

"I don't have much to say."

Her smile held the right amount of casual humor to appear friendly, but it was deceiving, he decided. Nothing about her invited a deeper relationship to develop.

The sun came up over the ridge that shaded the lodge long after the sky had brightened to blue. It fell across the table with sudden warmth and illuminated her face.

Before the glasses could darken completely, he stared into her startled gaze. His breath caught in his throat. She had the bluest eyes with the longest, blackest eyelashes he'd ever seen.

The blue irises turned the grayish hue of wood smoke as the light-sensitive lens darkened. She pushed the frame firmly against her nose as if to make sure her eyes were hidden.

"You have lovely eyes," he said. He couldn't look away.

Her mouth tightened, but she merely shrugged as if she couldn't care less.

He hesitated, knowing she didn't like questions, but his curiosity was piqued. "Why the shades? They don't appear to be prescription. Why do you wear them?"

"They keep the glare out of my eyes."

The answer was too quick, too practiced not to have been used before. "Uh-huh," he said. "And hide your thoughts?"

A true smile played around her mouth, fascinating him with the delicate line of her lips. He couldn't decide if their color was natural or not.

"I have no thoughts," she declared.

Not any that she cared to share, he deduced. He returned the slight smile and polished off the last bites of his breakfast.

She said nothing more as she finished her own meal. After taking her dishes to the kitchen and putting them in the dishwasher, she filled her mug with coffee and, to his surprise, returned to the table.

At least she didn't make a show of waiting on him and trying to please him as the boy-crazy college student employed earlier in the summer had done. She'd brought him no end of annoyance as he employed one evasive tactic after another until her finally let her go.

He didn't think he would have that problem with Mary. She bristled with invisible No Trespassing signs. A hum in his veins indicated he was maybe a tad disappointed at this assessment of the newly hired help, but he knew where the boundaries between boss and wrangler were drawn.

Rising, he bussed his place and refreshed his coffee, then resumed his seat. "There's a family near here," he said thoughtfully. "The next ranch over, in fact. Blue eyes and black hair run in their clan."

Through the dark lenses, he could see her

gaze fasten on his face, but not a whit of emotion came through.

She blew across the hot coffee, then took a sip. Setting the mug on the table, she gave him a wary glance, then looked past him to the outside. "It's a combination common to northern Italy. Also to some Irish, I think."

"Are you Irish?"

Her mouth tightened slightly, then relaxed. "I don't know anything about my ancestry."

"Your name sounds Irish."

"It was given to me." She shrugged. "They were at the M's in the alphabet."

"The orphanage," he murmured in understanding. "How old were you when you went there?"

"Around five, they decided."

He noted her choice of words. "Were your parents killed in an auto wreck or something?"

She was silent for a long moment. "I don't know what happened to my mother. My father abandoned me when I was three or four."

He tried to make the pieces fit together, but there was something he didn't understand. "Did you live with relatives for a year or two?"

Her smile was quick and genuine. "I lived with an old woman. She sort of adopted me, she and a boy who lived down the street. He's the one who found me sitting on the curb, crying. He took me to his neighbor because she always took in stray dogs and cats. I guess he thought I qualified as a stray, too."

"Then what happened?" he asked, intrigued by her story, which sounded like something from a movie rather than real life. He wondered at the parts she was leaving out...and even if her tale was true.

"They made sure I had food and clothing and went to the county health clinic for my shots. After a year or so, a neighbor turned me in because I wasn't going to school. The police handed me over to the juvenile authorities. A church group took an interest in my case and got me in an orphanage they sponsored."

"The place was also a working ranch?"

"Yes."

"Were you born in Wyoming?"

The delicate arch of her black eyebrows

lifted. "Well, that's what it says on my birth certificate."

He nodded and suppressed the other questions that rose to his tongue. This woman didn't like being interrogated.

Well, neither did he, come to think of it. He considered, paused, then said, "I had a cousin who stuttered after his mother died. Was that what happened to you after your father left you?"

For a second her face seemed set in stone, then she gave a shrug that expertly blended insouciance with defiance. "No, that was after they shaved my head at the orphanage."

A mixture of feelings ran through Jonah. Shock was foremost, and he'd have sworn nothing could shock him. "Why?" he demanded. "Why did they shave your head?"

"It was standard procedure for lice."

A beat of silence ensued.

"You're a survivor," he said and heard the rare note of admiration in his voice.

She laughed. "Aren't we all?"

When she rose, he did, too. "Our guests are up," he told her, hearing footsteps overhead.

"What am I supposed to do?"

"Help me set up a buffet. I don't serve hot breakfasts unless the temperature is freezing."

"Let them eat cake," she murmured, her expression behind the glasses impish.

The humor surprised him. He liked that as well as the courage and stoic resolve to survive indicated by her past, not to mention the sight of her incredibly long legs as she preceded him into the kitchen, the slender but definite curve of her hips and the way she carried herself—head up and shoulders level.

The hum of sexual interest increased to a roar. Huh. Maybe he'd better warn her to lock her door at night. Seeing the smiles the hungry men gave her as they piled into the dining room, he thought that was a good idea.

As soon as the buffet was set with plates, glasses, coffee mugs, a thermal container of coffee, plus various cereal boxes and the muffins, Mary scooted out the back door and down to the stables.

She checked the horses and mules in the paddock, saw Attila was happy with the group, then mucked out the stalls. Next, she stored the pitchfork and set about cleaning and oiling the tack, a job that obviously hadn't been done in ages. At the children's ranch where she'd grown up, they'd had to take good care of the stock and their gear since getting more had depended on the donations they received.

After conscientiously doing the ranch chores first, she did the same to her gear and stored it in the SUV.

Finally she tackled the horse trailer, cleaning it and laying the rubber mat out to dry in the shade of a very old oak whose leaves were starting to turn yellow.

A sign of winter, she thought, pausing to recover her strength after wrestling with the trailer mat made to withstand hundreds of pounds of pressure from shod hooves.

The westward peaks drew her attention. She stared at them while the oddest feelings raced around inside her.

Seven Devils.

Even the name set up a hot swirl of panic or something equally strange in the center of her being. She pressed a hand to her chest to still the tumult, but it seethed and roiled like the boiling mud pots she'd seen at Yellowstone once on her way north to the next rodeo.

The mountains and her new boss. They both bothered her in ways she couldn't describe.

Glad that the first job she'd been hurrying to fill hadn't worked out, she wondered if this one would and if she could stay long enough for Attila to heal. She would need to start his training all over again and bring him up to speed.

Being here at the ranch, where she received room and board, she could save nearly every penny of her salary, which was a dollar above minimum wage. Next summer she would head south and join the steeple circuit again. If Attila was well enough. If she could accumulate enough to pay for food, gas and fees. As usual, she'd sleep in the truck.

She handled her finances through an online bank. One thousand dollars stood between her and destitution at the present. Ah, well, she'd faced leaner times. After paying for the dun, she'd been down to counting pennies and collecting soda cans for recycling to stave off poverty, while she continued to work the race circuit in California for the rest of the season.

Shaking her head impatiently, she shoved the thoughts to the back of her mind and hurried to the lodge to see what she was supposed to do next. She hoped it was mending fences or something equally solitary.

"Can you change beds?" was the question that greeted her as soon as she walked in the door.

"Uh, as in change rooms?" she asked.

Jonah shook his head. "Change the sheets and make up the beds in the guest rooms. They'll also need dusting and checking for any lost items. Empty the wastebaskets, too."

"Sure."

Upstairs, she stripped the six beds, gathered the used towels and started the washing machine she'd discovered in a laundry/storage room yesterday while searching for the bathroom. Next to the laundry was a room with a large, tiled shower. A powder room with a toilet and sink was on the other side of that. Each bedroom also had its own sink, which was convenient for the occupants.

Linens and towels were stored in a cabinet

in the laundry room, which also held a vacuum cleaner and cleaning supplies. While the sheets were washing, she made up the beds with fresh ones, then cleaned and checked each room as instructed. By the time the second load of sheets was spinning out, she had the rooms finished.

She cleaned the shower and powder room, then vacuumed the hall runner. Finally she folded and stored the clean linens, then put fresh towels in all the rooms.

Noting the empty vases on the reading tables, she dashed outside and picked long stalks of dried grass beside the stable, plus a few graceful branches from a hemlock and a juniper. These she made into interesting arrangements in the vases in each guest room, then used the leftover pieces in her room.

"Very nice," a deep voice said from the doorway.

Startled, she jerked around. Her boss stood there, his expression thoughtful. She tried not to sound defensive as she explained, "I placed some grass and evergreens in all the guest rooms."

"Yeah, I saw them. Good idea."

She relaxed, unable to figure out what it was about him that made her nervous. Other than his ability to move around the place without a sound. And to probe her mind with a glance and a few observant questions.

"What's next?" she asked.

"Roundup. Keith and Janis are driving part of the herd this way. We'll meet them and bring the cattle here. The seed cows stay for the winter. The rest go to the stock sales or are delivered to those we have contracts with."

She detected a note of displeasure in his manner, but hadn't a clue to what bothered him. "Uh, who takes care of the campers? And the store?"

He shrugged. "We use the honor system. It seems to work okay most of the time."

"I can probably handle the herd—"

"You don't know where it is."

"I'm good at directions."

He studied her long enough to start the qualms to churning. He didn't have a lot of faith in her abilities. She met his gaze dead-on, determined to show him she could hold her own against any male wrangler.

"Do you always argue with the boss?" he demanded.

She'd asked for that one. "Not always." She kept her tone neutral.

"Just most of the time," he muttered, then he smiled. "The rooms look nice. It's time for lunch. We'll eat, then hit the trail."

"I'll need a mount."

"You'll need two for the country we'll be traveling. The horses should be rested enough to leave around one o'clock."

She nodded as a trill of excitement pinged around inside her like an echo in a box canyon. Actually she'd only herded animals a few times in her youth and at the rodeos where she'd usually helped with the bucking broncos.

No need to tell him that. Cattle were just critters. She could handle critters.

JONAH CLOSED THE safe and spun the cylinders. He'd bought the relic at his cousin's shop last year. Wells Fargo was still visible in faded gold letters on the front. It suited the resort's needs perfectly.

He liked things that fit in, that made sense

in the grand scheme of life as he saw it. He was pretty sure the new wrangler didn't fit any mold.

As a former orphan, she might not appreciate the intimacy of long winter days snowed in, just the two of them at the lodge when hunting season ended. You could get to know a person extremely well in those circumstances.

However, Keith and his family did come over if the weather got too bad to stay at their place. That added some diversity to the winter nights. After the new year began, the snowmobile and winter hiking crowd would show up.

She might not like that, either, he admitted. He'd already deduced that she preferred being around animals more than people. Interesting. In his experience, women loved any excuse to go to town and gossip with friends.

He wondered if she was running from something…or someone. Zack Dalton was the assistant sheriff. He could ask the lawman to check out her credentials.

A smile tweaked the seriousness of his thoughts. One thing—the lady could cook.

On a lot of ranches that would be enough to keep her at all costs.

He headed outside and spotted her at the fence. She had two cowponies saddled and two on leads. The rain gear and food packets he'd prepared after lunch were already tied behind the saddles or on the spare mounts.

"You're efficient," he commented.

"One learns to be."

"In the orphanage?"

"At the rodeo. You have to move things along for the shows. Broncos and bulls aren't always cooperative."

Her smile was brief, but intriguing as it hinted at memories of her past. He refrained from questions.

"Your horses are very well trained," she finished.

"Most of them are retired cutting horses. Our neighbors, the Daltons, raise and train some of the best. Keith and I buy the ones that are getting a bit long in the tooth."

"An old-age home for horses," she murmured. "I like that." She patted her mount's neck.

He noted she had her gloves on, but no

chaps. "You'll need chaps to get through some of the brush. There're extra pairs in the tack room."

She nodded and hurried to the stable. The tack room took up a space the size of a stall at one end. She returned in less than two minutes, the leather chaps outlining her body.

Watch it, he warned his libido as she swung up into the saddle, her lithe, slender body moving with sensuous ease. She was the hired hand and way, way off-limits to anything that might come to mind.

He glanced at the lofty mountain peaks surrounding the ranch. At present, there were only a couple of lingering ridges of last year's snow on the highest peak. The first snow of the current season hadn't fallen yet, but when it did, they could be snowed in for days at the lodge.

The question on his mind wasn't whether she could take it, but whether *he* could.

Startled, he glanced around as he headed across the pasture to a trail bordering a steep hill. She was gazing back at the main house as if memorizing the place.

Her T-shirt fit snugly across her chest, revealing the outlines of her bra and her small, pert breasts.

His blood surged with heat. This, he admitted wryly, wasn't the first time he'd been around a female wrangler, but it was the first time he'd reacted to one with intense male-to-female interest.

At thirty-four, he was sure of his control. After all, he'd been around beautiful women in abundance in New York, from top models in their fields to self-assured actresses and businesswomen to fresh-faced new talent just off the farm. He'd dealt with all of them as fairly and impartially as possible, looking only at their suitability for the job at hand. Or for a pleasant evening or weekend, no strings attached. He'd made sure his companions agreed with that philosophy. Marriage wasn't part of the package.

Following the new wrangler's gaze as she faced west and studied the famous mountains, he wondered if another snowbound winter on the ranch would change his mind. He smiled sardonically at the thought.

Chapter Three

Mary inhaled the balsam-scented air and decided she could stay here in this one place forever.

"Ready?" Jonah asked, rising from the boulder where he'd taken his rest. He tucked the remainder of the trail mix packet into his shirt pocket and took a swig of water from a plastic bottle.

"Yes," she said, also getting to her feet. She'd gobbled down all her snack as soon as they'd taken a break. She was still hungry, she realized.

"Hold still," he ordered.

She froze.

He smacked her on the back of her thigh, a glancing blow that startled her.

"What—" she began.

"A tick. You have to watch for them if

you're going to sit on a log. Turn around. Slowly."

She followed his directions.

"Okay, I don't see any others."

Creepy-crawly sensations ran over her skin. She brushed vigorously at the back of her jeans, down her legs, then along her shirt-sleeves just to be sure the little buggers hadn't hitched a ride in a fold of fabric.

"Makes you feel as if you have a thousand of 'em on you, doesn't it?"

She looked up to find him grinning at her precautions and nodded. With an effort, she refrained from whipping her hat off, releasing her braids and running her fingers all over her scalp, which now felt under attack from un-seen little beasties with a thousand legs each.

"You're okay," he assured her, then laughed as she felt along her neck.

They mounted and headed out again. She wondered how long they would follow the steep game trail through the silent forest. They'd been riding for more than an hour and had crossed two ridges.

The answer came when the downward path opened into a meadow nearly an hour later.

A carpet of white and yellow fall flowers landscaped the area. Cattle dotted the land, munching on the sparse grass and abundant flowers.

"Ah," her boss said, "there's Keith."

She spotted the lone cowboy circling the far side of the herd. He waved his hat to indicate he saw them, too, then urged his mount to a faster pace.

Jonah waved, then reined up in front of a cabin built on a hillock overlooking the five-acre meadow. He dismounted, tied his two cowponies to a tree and indicated she should do the same.

"Are we spending the night here?" she asked, perusing the cabin which couldn't possibly be more than one room. Would it hold three people?

"You are," Jonah answered as she dismounted and tied her horse and spare cowpony next to his.

"Hey," Keith Towbridge called, arriving at the cabin. He dismounted and dropped the reins, leaving his horse ground-hitched a few feet from theirs. "Glad to see you guys," he added, smiling at Jonah, then surveying her.

Mary held out her hand. "Mary McHale, the wrangler," she introduced herself.

"Keith Towbridge," he answered and shook hands. He turned to his partner. "Everything looks good around here. There's a young bear over near the Dalton line shack. He's ventured this way a couple of times, but he's no problem."

"Cats?" Jonah asked.

Keith shook his head. "No signs of any. One was spotted over at the canyon last week. Scared a couple of vacationers in their camp, but it seemed mostly curious."

"What's the count?" Jonah next asked.

"Fifty-two mamas, fifty-eight babies."

"Better than last year," her boss said in pleased tones.

Mary listened to the report while she sized up the two men. Keith was about her height and her age, she thought. He looked younger than Jonah, who she judged to be in his early to mid-thirties. A wedding band reminded her that Keith was married and had a son.

"I'm heading home for the night," the younger man told them. "We have a dozen head of cattle there. Janis and I'll bring them over tomorrow. You two staying here?"

Jonah shook his head. "I thought I'd head back since we have several campers checking out today and more in the morning. Mary can keep an eye on the herd while you bring in the other cattle tomorrow. I'll be back in the afternoon or first thing Thursday morning to drive them down the valley."

Keith gave his partner a sharp glance, then turned to her. "You okay with being here alone?"

Mary nodded. Actually she was relieved.

"There's food and firewood in the cabin," Keith told her. "Nothing will bother you."

"I'll be fine," she said, smiling to show she wasn't worried about the solitude.

"She prefers her own company," Jonah informed his partner rather dryly.

"Actually I just like the quiet," she said to Keith, ignoring Jonah and his conclusions about her.

"You'll do," Keith said with an approving grin at her and a speculative glance at Jonah. "See you tomorrow."

She and Jonah watched him mount and

head southwest. In a minute he disappeared into the trees. "Anything in particular I should know about the cattle?" she asked.

"No. Just keep an eye on them. There's a creek near here. We'll water the horses, then I'll lay a fire in the stove and show you where everything is."

She followed his example in caring for their mounts, leaving her ponies hobbled in the meadow with the herd while he switched his saddle to his spare. He went into the cabin.

Mary observed from the door while he laid pine cones, kindling and wood in the old-fashioned iron stove set on a hearth of field stones at one end of the cabin. "Matches," he said, holding up the box to show her. After she nodded, he replaced them on the shelf mounted on the wall.

He pointed to one side of the wood stacked in a corner. "Old newspapers, in case you need them to get the fire started. Sometimes it's hard to get the stovepipe to draw."

"You have to heat the cold air to get an updraft going," she said to let him know she understood how to start a blaze in the pot-bellied stove.

Two double bunks, stacked on opposite walls, offered resting places for four people, she noted.

"Blankets," Jonah said, removing the top from a barrel. He tossed three of them on one of the bunkbeds. "There's soup, crackers, a can opener." He pointed out the items.

She nodded.

He eyed her for a minute, then told her to wait. He went outside, then returned with a pistol. "You won't need this, but keep it handy anyway. Just in case."

"Just in case of what?"

He raised one black eyebrow as if impatient with the question. "In case you need to scare off a nosy bear or mountain cat. Or a rustler or two."

A frisson jolted down her spine. She hoped no one came around while she was there.

Jonah studied her again. "The idea of bears and pumas doesn't seem to bother you, but having humans around does. Why is that?"

"Well, I've never shot anybody before," she admitted.

"Have you ever fired a gun?"

"No."

He gave a grunt that said he'd expected as much. Moving close, he showed her the pistol and how it worked. When he was satisfied she understood how to use the weapon, he laid it on the bunk with the blankets. "Keep it close. It won't go off accidentally," he added. "It has a heavy pull."

She had a sudden image of a man holding a gun. Standing in the shadows, she'd watched while the man who might have been her father had jumped into his pickup and driven out of the parking lot, throwing gravel in an arc behind the tires.

The man with the gun had gone back inside the building while she stayed perfectly still so he wouldn't see her. She'd remained behind the garbage cans when the door had closed behind him and finally fell asleep there, waiting for her father to come back for her.

"What is it?" a voice broke into her thoughts.

"What is what?" she asked.

"Are you scared to stay here?"

She shook her head. "I was just thinking of something. Something that happened a long time ago," she said when he continued to observe her. She returned his stare, aware of defiance rising in her. "You're looking at me the way one of my schoolteachers did, with that 'I don't know what you did, but I know you're guilty' expression."

His piercing stare eased. "She must have been related to one of my teachers. She thought anybody with Indian blood must be up to no good."

"You're Native American?"

"An eighth. My scalping tendencies have been diluted to only a twinge now and then."

She burst into laughter at the sarcastic remark.

"What?" he demanded.

"I tried to get a scalping party together once, but no one would join in. I wanted to shave off the principal's hair the same as he did to new kids in the school."

Mary stopped smiling as a mixture of emotion, too fast to read, swept over Jonah's features. "That was a mean thing to do to kids," he said.

"Yes, it was. But I suppose it was a cheap way to solve the problem."

She stopped the words with an effort,

aware of his keen gaze on her, assessing every nuance, every weakness she disclosed. She hated being the least bit vulnerable, but she couldn't look away…couldn't move…

He held her glance while he took one step closer. When he reached out and removed her hat, tossing it on one of the bunks without a glance, she remained where she was although everything in her said she should run…*run*.

With a deft touch, he removed the two long hairpins, then the stretchy band that held her braid securely.

"Don't," she said, but the word came out feeble, more like a gasp than a protest.

"It's okay," he said as if soothing an animal. "I just want to look. I won't hurt you."

She felt her hair fall around her shoulders and to a point at her waist as he loosened the thick strands. Finally he ran his fingers through the long mass from her scalp to the ends.

Like a rabbit too frightened to move, she stood there, heart pounding, while he looked his fill. When he removed her glasses and laid them on the rough wooden table behind him, she didn't utter a sound.

"Beautiful," he said, a note of wonder in his voice. He gathered a fistful of her hair in his hand.

Like the child she'd once been, she felt helpless while others scrutinized and talked about her as if she couldn't hear their hurting, insulting words. Shards of old pain and anger swept through her. She knocked his hand away and took a defensive step backward.

He blinked as if coming out of a trance and muttered a low curse. "I'm sorry," he at once apologized, shoving his hands into the pockets of his jeans. "I didn't mean to upset you. I've never touched an unwilling woman in my life."

The anger in his eyes was real and directed at himself, she realized. With a stiff nod, she accepted the apology.

His frown smoothed out as he moved back, putting some distance between them. "I must admit I've never been mesmerized by a woman, either. That dark hair combined with those blue eyes is a stunning combination."

She twisted the unkempt locks into a bun

and crushed her hat over the lot before it could fall in unruly waves around her face. With her glasses in place, she felt safe once more.

"I can see why you hide behind those," he said, his manner wise but sardonic at the same time. "Like the sirens calling to the Argonauts, no mere man can long withstand the temptation—"

"I'm not a siren," she interrupted hotly. "I don't try to attract anyone's attention."

"Honey, you don't have to try," he told her softly. With a shake of his head, he walked out the door, leaving it open as he left. "I'll see you tomorrow."

Mary went outside, tense and alert until he rode out of sight. He'd left his earlier mount hobbled with the other two horses. She wondered if he would have stayed the night had she been a cowboy instead of a cowgirl and if that odd episode hadn't taken place inside the tight quarters of the cabin.

The tension eased out of her shoulders. Some instinct deep inside said that she could trust him. Over the years, she'd learned to rely on her instincts about a person.

Once it had saved her from one of the seedy

men who always seemed to hang around the racetracks looking for a sure tip on a winner. He'd trapped her in a stall, but had backed away quick enough when she'd calmly faced him, sharp tines of a pitchfork pointing directly at him, and gave him a cool smile that said she would be delighted to run him through.

Taking a seat on a boulder as she perused the peaceful scene in the meadow, she laid her hat aside and massaged her scalp, her thoughts centered on the cabin and her boss.

His hands had been strong when he'd showed her how to fire the gun, his fingers lean and purposeful as he demonstrated the correct technique on the trigger. But he'd been so very gentle when he'd gathered her hair into his fist and brushed the ends against his chin.

Mixed emotions—longing, caution, old hurts—tangled into a knot in her belly. Leaping to her feet, she saddled her spare mount and rode around the meadow, moving the cattle into a closer bunch as twilight shadowed the landscape.

She wouldn't be foolish, she vowed. She was never foolish. No one got to her, not now, not ever.

JONAH FINISHED COUNTING up the receipts and checked the total against the cash and credit card charges. They were the same. Good.

Yawning he closed out the accounting program on the computer, locked the safe, then went into the sun room adjoining the tiny office. After closing the curtains on the bank of windows that lined three walls, he undressed, showered in the tiny bathroom and was in bed by five after eleven.

Usually he fell asleep pretty fast, but tonight his mind stubbornly traveled down a path of its own choosing.

Mary McHale. Wrangler. Orphan. Self-sufficient loner. And one of the most beautiful women he'd ever seen.

A jolt in his heartbeat coupled with the warmth that poured down his body warned him of Danger with a capital D.

He didn't want involvement of any kind, emotional or sexual. He'd been there, done that and got the broken heart to prove it.

Five years ago in New York he'd met another beautiful woman, but his dreams of them had been doomed from the start. She'd come from a small Southern town and had loved the bright lights of the city and the excitement to be found at any hour of the day or night. She'd spurned his offer of marriage and a simple life in the suburbs with two kids and a dog.

So much for romantic dreams, love conquers all and the rest of that fantasy. When the chance had come to leave the Big Apple and establish a life here in the back country, he'd done so without a second thought.

So why was he thinking of the past now?

Mary McHale. He'd seen her standing and staring at the western peaks as if her heart was impaled on those sharp points. She might think he ran an old-age home for cowponies, but he sure as hell wasn't running a refuge for the walking wounded. Whatever her problems, they were her own, not his.

He gave a cynical snort. Life had a way of catching up with a person, though, and having the last laugh. He was attracted to her taut slenderness, the way she moved, going from one task to another with a calm efficiency that got things done.

And there was that unexpected sense of humor peeking impishly through the defensive poise. He liked that best of all. Before he went to sleep, he wondered again if she would stay through the winter.

"HELLO-O-O."

Mary went outside to see who had arrived. Keith Towbridge, and a child in a cloth carrier on the saddle in front of him, entered the meadow from the trail through the trees. Another rider followed close behind. A woman. They drove a dozen cattle toward the herd.

"Hi," Mary called. "You're just in time for lunch."

"Good. The monster is hungry," the woman said with a smile. "I'm Janis. You must be Mary."

"That's right. Is this K.J.?"

"Yeah. Can you grab him?" Keith asked.

Before Mary quite grasped what was happening, the toddler had been thrust into her arms. She settled him on her left hip and gave him a smile. "Hey, little man."

He stuck a finger in his mouth and stared at her with eyes that were starting to change from the universal baby-blue to green and brown shades.

Since the older kids had helped with the younger children at the orphanage, she had experience with the way a baby could level an unblinking stare at a person as if looking into one's soul. She grinned and clicked her tongue at the child.

He grinned back and tapped her cheek with damp fingers.

Janis laughed as she dismounted and handed the reins to her husband. "The Daltons taught him that. They greet him with a high five all the time so he thinks he's supposed to smack everyone he meets. My sister is married to Zack, so we see the whole gang frequently."

Mary nodded politely. The Daltons were neighbors, Jonah had told her.

"You have any trouble with the cattle?" Keith asked after tying their horses in the shade.

"None. It was quiet around here." She gestured to the cabin. "I'm heating soup. Would you like some?"

Both adults nodded. The baby waved his arms as if he approved the idea of eating, bringing laughter to the adults.

Mary carried him inside, then turned him over to his mom while she added another can of soup to the pan on the stove, set out crackers and opened two cans of Vienna sausage and two of mixed fruit to go with their meager fare.

Keith came inside carrying a diaper bag. Soon they were eating. Janis expertly spooned food into K.J., ate and talked at same time. She told Mary about the ranch house they were renovating and the funny things that happened with the city dudes who didn't know one end of a horse from the other.

Keith confided to Mary, "Neither did she when I brought her to the ranch a year ago last spring."

"I learned fast," she declared.

"You did," he agreed.

His glance at Janis was pure adoration. It caused Mary's heart to thump hard against her ribs. She didn't think anyone had ever gazed at her like that.

"Tell her about your background," he finished with a grin at his pretty wife, who had green eyes and light brown hair with blond streaks that Mary thought had really come from being out in the sun.

Janis wrinkled her nose. "My father's a senator. He's running for governor of the state. Since the election is in November, the race is heating up. You'll see him on the local TV newscasts every night."

"And his wife and two daughters every chance the reporters get to sneak in and film some footage," Keith added.

"The difference is," Janis continued, "that my mom loves campaigning and all that. Alison and I don't. I warned Keith before we married that it might be this way."

He shrugged. "It doesn't matter." He smiled at Mary. "Just don't be surprised if a camera pops up in your face one day and some nosy reporter demands you tell everything you know about us."

"What do you do when that happens?" Mary asked.

"Ignore them," Janis advised. "Tell 'em you're new here and don't know anything about the family."

Mary hoped she wouldn't have to face that dilemma.

"So, where are you from?" Janis asked.

Mary figured Jonah would tell them the basic facts about her, so she gave them a brief summary of her life.

"Uncle Nick knows a lot about horses," Keith said after she'd explained about Attila's injury.

Janis agreed. "Also his nephews. Zack and the twins do all the training of their cowponies. They know everything about injuries and physical therapy for horses."

Mary recognized the uncle's name. "Uh, the Daltons who live on the next ranch?"

"Yes," Keith said. "You know them?"

"No. Jonah mentioned them."

"The eyes," Janis said suddenly. "It's the eyes. You have eyes the exact same shade of blue that the Daltons have. All of them except Seth."

Mary realized her shades were lying on the shelf where she'd put them after coming inside from the sunlight to find something for lunch. She'd forgotten to put them on when the couple arrived. "My father's eyes were blue," she said, not having the least idea if this was true, but feeling a need to say something, as if she had to defend herself.

"They're really beautiful," Janis said with no trace of envy. "Hey, man, are you through eating?" she asked her son.

"Mmmmff," he replied, then yawned hugely.

Janis tickled him under the chin. "We need to get home. It's nearly time for his afternoon nap."

After the others were on their way, Mary stood at the door, her sunglasses safely on her face, and watched them go. A happy family, she thought, and tried not to notice the empty pang that stabbed her in the vicinity of her heart. She'd done quite a bit of babysitting over the years. Babies were nice. They didn't ask questions.

After riding around the herd once more and doing another count to be sure none of the cattle had strayed into the forest, she explored a trickle of water that flowed into the little creek, one that she'd noticed the day before.

As she'd suspected, when she traced it to its source, it came from a spring, not just any spring, but a hot spring. A faint swirl of steam rose from the surface of a little pool where the water collected before plunging over a three-foot rocky ledge and winding its way to the creek.

She glanced around and listened hard. Only the random twittering of birds and an occasional *moo* from a cow greeted her ears. She ground-hitched the horse, then tested the water with her finger. Just right.

After checking around once more, she swirled her hand through the pool to make sure it wasn't deceptively pleasant on the surface and hot—or cold—in the deeper part.

It was perfect.

She stripped her clothing, hung everything neatly on a nearby branch, hesitated, then loosened her hair. She'd been wanting to scrub it since Jonah had found the tick on her the day before.

Sliding into the pool, she heaved a sigh of contentment. Ah, bliss…

JONAH FOUND THE herd resting peacefully when he arrived Wednesday afternoon, but the new wrangler wasn't anywhere in sight. His horse greeted the other two in the meadow. From the trees, he heard an answering whicker. He dismounted, tied up and walked toward the woods bordering the creek.

Stopping in the deep shade, Jonah spotted Mary's horse munching some mossy plants to one side. He circled around and walked beside the tiny creek that flowed into the main one that ran through the meadow.

Wisps of steam rose from the pool. At first he didn't see anything unusual, then a vision rose from the depths, showering water like crystal gems all around.

He froze as Mary stood in the hip-deep water, black hair cascading down her back as she swept it from her face. He got a glimpse of smooth shoulders and the delicate indentation of her spine, of slender hips and nice curves.

And a tattoo of a unicorn high on her thigh.

His mouth went dry. His breath stuck in his throat. Blood pounded furiously through every part of him. As she started to turn, he knew he had to move. Fast.

Stepping behind a thick juniper, he backed away until he was at the edge of the woods.

"Hello," he called after forcing air into his lungs once more. "Anyone here?"

"Don't come any closer," Mary called out in warning.

He managed a laugh. "You in the hot tub?"

"Uh, yes. I'm…I thought I'd wash my hair."

"Right. I'll see you back at the cabin."

"Yes. I'll be there in just a minute."

He hurried to the line shack and waited, his gaze moving automatically over the herd. His heart rate was nearly back to normal when the wrangler rode up a few minutes later.

As usual, her hair was hidden under the hat, her eyes behind the sunglasses. Her plaid shirt was damp in places. The T-shirt that she'd used as a towel was draped over the pommel.

"Things were quiet," she said, dismounting and tying up her horse. "I thought I would take a quick bath."

"I've never met anyone yet who could resist the hot springs. Around here, everyone calls it the cowboy's bathtub." He saw the tension ease from her shoulders as he kept up the humorous chatter.

"I was worried I might get boiled, but the

water was perfect. Ever since you spotted the tick on me, I've been desperate to wash my hair."

"You'd better take your hat off and let it dry in the sun. My mom always said you shouldn't go to bed with damp hair. She never mentioned what would happen as a consequence, but from her tone it must be terrible."

He was surprised by Mary's laughter, a soft murmur of sound that was too brief.

"The housemother used to say the same thing," she added. She gestured toward the cattle. "Are we going to drive them to the lodge pastures today?"

"Yeah. You ready?"

"Yes. I've cleaned up the cabin, so it can be closed. Uh, here's your gun. I didn't have to shoot any bears or rustlers, thank goodness."

He stored the gun in his saddlebag, then gave the cabin a quick survey to make sure they hadn't forgotten anything. It was immaculate. Conscientious as well as efficient, he added to the list of her virtues.

"Let's move 'em out," he said, swinging into the saddle.

"I'll ride drag." She headed to the back of the herd to keep the laggards in line.

He took the lead, swinging a coiled rope to get the lazy cattle moving down the canyon trail. They would follow the downward flow of the creek until the land opened into a wide, flat valley that meandered around the steep ridge he and Mary had crossed the previous day.

Once the herd was moving at a steady pace, he rode around the perimeter to help the new wrangler keep a stubborn cow and her five cohorts from making a break for the wild country.

"We'll be going through a pass in a half hour. When the first deep snow falls, this area will be impassable until spring."

"Can Janis and Keith get out?" she asked.

He nodded. "There's another road to the main county one, plus a back way over to the Dalton place."

"The other road, does it have a one-lane wooden bridge?"

"Yes. Sounds as if you found it."

"I realized I'd turned too soon when I came

to the bridge and it wasn't on the map your cousin sketched on your camping brochure."

"Another three miles and you would have come to the Towbridge homestead. It's a rough road. We haven't had time to grade it this year. No one uses it as a rule."

The stubborn old cow made a break for it. Mary's cowpony headed it off before it reached the trees. Jonah held back the critters who would have followed by circling around them and directing them into the main herd. He noted the ease with which Mary stayed in the saddle, her lithe body moving in perfect concert with the horse.

He frowned as another image came to mind—one in which she stood as she had in the pool, sparkling drops falling from her body as she turned toward him, a smile of welcome on her face as he hurried to join her…

The pain of swift hard passion speared through him. He had a feeling that accidental vision was going to haunt him for a long time…long after the reticent wrangler left for warmer parts and easier work.

"Hey, get in there!" she yelled, laughter riffling her voice as she engaged the belligerent cow in a standoff.

No matter which way the cow turned, the horse and rider were there before it could get past them and into the trees.

Jonah relaxed in the saddle and watched the expert display of horsemanship. She was good, damned good. A natural with animals. He wondered if she'd last until Christmas.

But then, he hadn't thought Keith's wife, a city girl, could withstand the rigors of ranch life, but she'd surprised him. This woman seemed born to it.

An odd yearning filled him. He tried to analyze it, but the feeling defied rational examination. An aunt, who liked to tell fortunes, had told him he would someday experience a great love that would last the rest of his life. His gaze went to Mary as his heart rate went up—

His horse raced after a young bull that broke from the herd, startling him out of the introspection. He realized he'd better concentrate on the task at hand, or else his wrangler would show him up.

Chapter Four

Twilight covered the land in deep shadow when Mary drove the last of the herd through the gate Jonah had opened. The creek trail, while easier than the one over the steep ridges, had been much longer.

Her boss yelled "Good job," to her, closed the gate, then headed for the stable with his horse and the two spares. She stayed on her mount, letting it follow the others.

At the stable, she found her legs trembled when she stood on her own. She couldn't remember the last time she'd stayed in the saddle so long, and never while traversing land so rough in places she'd marveled that the cattle could make it without breaking a leg on the rocks that lined the trail.

But they had, and now they were safe in the home pastures. The breeding herd would stay here through the winter. Part of her job would be to feed them from the huge store of hay in the shed and protect them from predators.

Then spring would come and with it, new life—calves and grass and wildflowers. The mountains would be magnificent in the springtime.

"Go inside," a voice broke into her musing.

She blinked up at Jonah.

"Go on. You're beat. Take a shower and put on something comfortable. There's enough leftover soup for our supper."

She wanted to protest, but he removed the reins from her trembling fingers and sent her on her way.

In the lodge, she smiled at a couple shopping in the tiny store and continued up the stairs. She went straight to the shower room, undressed and thoroughly shampooed and soaped all over, then rinsed in the luxurious warmth. She checked for ticks and, thank heavens, didn't find any.

A little of the fatigue eased once she was dressed in a clean sweat suit with thick socks to cushion her feet. She dried her hair, pulled it through a scrunchy band, then hesitated over the glasses.

She left them on the chest of drawers in her room and padded down the stairs. The couple were adding up their purchase. "Here's your money," the man told her. He placed some bills in a box on the counter.

"Do you need change?" she asked.

"No, we're fine."

They gathered their purchases and left. She continued to the kitchen. From there, she could hear water running through the pipes and assumed Jonah was also taking a shower.

An image came to her—him smiling and holding out a hand to invite her inside the steamy shower. His body would be lean and powerful, his touch gentle...

She blinked, startled by the vision. It had been a long time since she'd let anyone breach her defenses. When she'd first left the orphanage and gotten work at a rodeo, she'd fallen hard for a handsome bull rider, but then she'd found out he was engaged to a wealthy rancher's daughter. He'd seemed to think they could continue with their affair.

The pain of being eighteen and believing in

love and promises swirled through her. She'd learned that men responded to the physical, especially her dark hair and blue eyes, the slight cleft in her chin and the dimple that appeared when she truly smiled.

So she'd hidden her hair and eyes and quit smiling.

For an insane moment she wished she were starting over in life, as trusting and eager for adventure as a spring lamb. Then she shrugged and set about heating two bowls of soup in the microwave oven. After preparing a glass of chocolate milk, she sipped it as she leaned against the counter, her eyes on the western hills, which were barely discernible shadows against the sky.

Her mind was oddly blank, as if in blinking out Jonah's image and memories of the past, she'd closed off the thinking part of her brain.

When the microwave dinged, she straightened, but Jonah, also in socks, was there before she could move. "Go sit down," he ordered, but in a kind, gruff voice.

She went into the dining room and sat at the table they'd shared the previous day. He brought out the soup and thick ham sandwiches with lettuce and delicious tomato slices. When she exclaimed over the flavor, he told her they were homegrown.

"The season is nearly over, but we'll go to town toward the end of next week and see what they have in the farmer's market. The corn has been really good this year."

"Is the market in Lost Valley?"

He nodded.

"It seemed like a nice place when I came through. I gassed up at the station there and had lunch in a diner."

"The diner is new," he told her. "The area is growing, which delights the town council, but I don't like it. I left New York to get away from traffic."

"I think it will be a while before the town annexes the ranch into its city limits." She smiled at his mock-worried expression and asked about his life in the city.

After his brief bio, she said, "It's hard to imagine a person giving up New York and Madison Avenue for Idaho and the Seven Devils Mountains."

He raised one eyebrow and studied her. "Well, you gave up the life of a short-order cook to be a cowgirl. I don't see that my choice was all that different."

His smile flashed brilliantly white against his tanned face, drawing another smile from her. She realized she'd smiled, even laughed, more in the past two days than she had in two years, or three, or four...

"You should do that more often," he murmured.

"What?"

"Smile."

Without giving her time to withdraw behind her curtain of caution, he stood and carried their dishes to the kitchen.

"Sit still. I'll bring you a cup of tea," he called out.

A strange heat spread through her. Now that she'd eaten, her energy was renewed, but she felt tremors of a different kind tingling through her muscles. She wasn't used to being waited on, and she wasn't sure she liked it.

Neither did she like the heat of attraction that spread through her clear down to her toes. She might not be able to stay here, after all. A winter alone with Jonah could prove too dangerous. She didn't want to embarrass herself by drooling over him, she added with caustic humor.

When he returned with two cups of herbal tea, she perused him with quick, sideways glances, edgy about being alone with him, no one at the lodge but the two of them.

"I'm not going to pounce on you," he said quietly, a flicker of humor in the words. He resumed his seat. "That doesn't mean I don't want to, but I won't."

She stared at him, mouth agape.

He laughed, another temptation in itself, his voice smooth and luxuriously deep. "Drink up, cowgirl, then go to bed. You've had a long day. By morning, you'll have all your fences in place again."

"This is so strange," she said, talking more to herself than to him.

His eyes roamed over her face as if memorizing its planes and shapes. "Not so strange. You're a very beautiful woman. And I still have warm blood flowing through my veins."

Her lips trembled when she tried to smile to show she knew he was teasing her.

However, he didn't smile. While he continued his intense study, she did the same to him, noting the moody darkness now in his eyes and a slight puzzlement in his manner.

Oddly it didn't upset her, although it made her a bit nervous, not of him but her own wayward interest and heated blood. The vision of his wet, naked body returned, setting off a rage of hunger inside her. She wanted desperately to be held, caressed, kissed. She could almost feel his lips on hers, gentle, demanding but giving, too.

Her breath became uneven. She stood, knowing she had to flee before she came apart, before he recognized the longing in her blood.

He stood at the same instant.

"I should go," she said in breathless, defensive tones.

"Yes."

His voice was deep, husky, a glissade of sound so seductive her knees would have buckled had she not grabbed the chair. With two steps, he was at her side. He laid the tips of his fingers against her cheek as if testing that she was real.

"Who are you?" he said. "Who are you really?"

She shook her head, unable to think of an answer.

He bent his head, and she stood there, knowing what was coming, knowing she should go, but unable to deny herself this one moment, to resist this one temptation.

His lips were warm, soft and dry. They drifted over hers with the sweetest movements, soothing and stirring at the same time. When she opened her mouth, unable to stop the response, his tongue glided between her lips.

She clutched the chair with one hand and clenched the other against her stomach as the world spun around and around and around in crazy splendor. Sensations sizzled through every nerve.

The kiss went on and on. When he lifted his head, she gave a faint moan and reached upward, wanting his mouth again.

"Go," he whispered hoarsely. "Now!"

She fled.

Long after she'd run down the hall and up the stairs, long after she'd locked the door behind her, long after she'd turned out the light, she lay in the comfortable bed and worried about the wisdom of lingering this close to temptation. With brutal honesty, she accepted the fact that she found him handsome and beguiling, and that she wanted more than kisses from him.

But, as he'd indicated, that didn't mean either of them had to act on the temptation. After all, they had stopped before anything other than a kiss had happened. They hadn't even put their hands on each other.

He was right. By morning she'd be fine, all her barriers up and in good shape once more.

THURSDAY, FRIDAY AND Saturday were three of the busiest days in recent experience, Mary decided, closing the stock gate from horseback, a trick she'd learned from watching her boss. He did nearly everything for the cows from the saddle, even administering medicine at times.

He was one of the best bosses she'd ever had. He told her exactly what was to be done, he showed her how to do it, then he let her get on with the task. She liked that.

There was only one flaw in this paradise. She was intensely sensitive to his physical presence when he was around and equally aware of the moments he wasn't. It was odd because she couldn't recall missing anyone—

Not that she missed him, she reminded herself sharply as she groomed her cowpony and put him out to pasture upon returning to the ranch headquarters late Saturday afternoon.

Jonah had trusted her to bring the small herd down from the upper pasture alone this time. She and Keith had rounded up another dozen head in the rough country north of the upper meadow. He'd returned home to his wife and son, and she'd started the cattle down the creek trail. Riding a well-trained cutting horse had made the job a pleasure and an easy task.

After petting Attila, who'd come running as soon as he caught her scent on the wind, she headed for the house. At the back door, she froze.

Jonah must have invited guests over. It sounded as if there was a party going on in the great room. She had to fight an urge to bolt for the stable again.

Instead she headed for the stairs as quickly

as possible on the theory that if she was fast enough, they might not notice her.

"Hi," her boss said, spotting her sneaking past the office. He held the phone to his shoulder. "Can you get the store? I'm tied up here."

She nodded and made her way through the throng of people—there were at least twenty guests—into the store. Another five were in the grocery, waiting to check out.

Glancing out the window, she spied several RVs in the campgrounds. She hadn't expected the resort part of the ranch to be this busy after the Labor Day weekend was over.

"Find everything okay?" she asked the first customer in line, putting on a polite smile.

"Well," the lady said, "you're out of the little salt and pepper shakers, but the woman behind me volunteered to share since she got the last ones, so I'm fine."

"I have plenty, too," another woman, who was there with her two children, spoke up. "Also flour and sugar and things like that. I restocked before we left home."

"Where y'all from?" the second woman in line asked.

Soon the three women were chatting like old friends. The two kids, a boy and a girl, were pleased to find out there was another boy their age in camp. Before Mary had finished adding up the bills on the calculator, they'd agreed to pool their resources and have a potluck dinner.

"Happy eating," she said when they all trooped out, still chatting merrily and exchanging information on the best camping places, easy recipes and treatment for bug bites. She grimaced as she faced the crowded great room again.

"Once more into the fray," she muttered and made a dash for the stairs.

"Mary, hold up," Jonah called out.

She stopped on the first step and turned to him.

"Hey, everybody," he said in a voice that carried over the laughter.

The crowd hushed and turned as one to them. Mary stared into a sea of faces. Most of the women had long, braided hair. About half the men wore theirs that way, too. She recognized one face.

"Hi," Trek Lanigan from the Trading Post said to her.

She smiled and nodded.

"This is Mary McHale, the new wrangler," Jonah said, laying a hand on her shoulder. "Be careful. She's rough, she's tough, and she don't take sass from anyone."

Mary was so horrified she could only stare at Jonah. He gave her a wink. The guests burst into guffaws.

"Mary, this is my family on the Native American side. My grandfather, Antonio Scout. My mother, Eva Rose Lanigan."

He then went on to name every uncle, aunt and cousin without a pause, including two babies being nursed by their respective mothers. The family applauded when he finished.

Mary smiled and murmured hello to the group. She would have raced up the steps except Jonah didn't release his hold on her. When she shied away a bit, his clasp tightened.

"We're celebrating my grandfather's birthday," he told her. "Dinner will be ready in fifteen minutes. That's plenty of time for you to shower and change, isn't it?"

"Uh, I'll grab a sandwich and eat in my room."

"My mother's feelings will be hurt. She's going to fix fry bread for everyone. Isn't that right, Madre?"

"Yes," the woman said. "The meal is nearly ready and you must eat, anyway. We would like for you to join us if you aren't too tired."

Mary felt it would be rude to refuse, so she nodded. Jonah gave her an approving glance and released her.

Upstairs, she showered and shampooed as quickly as possible. In her room she blow-dried her hair. Standing in front of the mirror in clean underwear, she studied her reflection like an artist looking for cracks in a statue.

When her hair had been short, it had also been curly. Once it grew out again, its weight straightened the curls into soft waves. Other than trimming the ends herself, she'd never let anyone get near her hair with scissors or a razor. Now it hung to her waist like a thick dark curtain.

She pinched a layer of skin over her ribs. Not much padding there. Her bra was an A cup. Not much there, either.

At times during the past week she'd caught Jonah gazing at her with a certain male-female interest that rattled her. She wasn't sure he even realized it.

She tried to see herself through his eyes, but wasn't sure what attracted a man to a woman.

From movies and magazines, it was pretty clear that big breasts and a sexy attitude were requisite. She didn't qualify on either count. Men liked long hair, though. And her eyes were nice, too. People had always commented on them.

It came to her that for the first time since she was eighteen she was thinking of attracting a man.

She frowned as worry nicked two little lines between her eyes. *Stop it,* she warned her libido or whatever part of a woman coaxed her to do foolish things. She was only staying at the ranch for a few months, then she would be on her way with Attila. There was no earthly reason to think of anything but her own plans.

Irritated with herself, she donned fresh jeans and a long-sleeved shirt, rolled the cuffs up on her arms, then braided her hair so tight she had to start over to ease the tension at her temples.

At the last second she added a pair of dream-catcher earrings and a dab of lipstick. With the usual thick socks to keep her feet warm as the evening cooled, she decided she didn't need shoes.

No one noticed her slip down the steps and hallway to the kitchen. "What can I do to help?" she asked Jonah and his mother, both busy with food.

"We'll set up a buffet in the dining room and let folks help themselves," he said, glancing up, then pausing and going over her from head to foot. "You look very nice," he murmured.

His mother removed fry bread from the skillet and gazed at Mary before pouring the next batch in. Then she looked at Jonah. Her eyes were dark gray, fathomless and very wise.

She was average in height, but gave an impression of being tall, perhaps due to her slender build. Her face was ageless, the skin drawn tight over the bones with few lines.

With a son in his thirties, Mary thought the other woman must be in her fifties although she looked closer to forty. She hoped, as time passed, that she aged so well.

She felt the heat sweep her face and neck as the woman smiled at her while she stared like a bumpkin. She grabbed a huge bowl of salad and took it to the dining room. There, she found the three tables pushed together for form one long serving counter. Vintage-style floral cloths covered them in bright colors.

Two teenage girls smiled shyly at her. "Hi, Mary," one said. "I'm Julianne. This is my cousin, Pam."

"Nice to meet you," Mary said. "Where do you want the salad?"

For the next ten minutes she and the girls worked together in setting up the buffet. When she asked where they lived and where they went to school and what their favorite subject was, the teenagers lost their inhibitions.

"Pam's favorite subject is boys," Julianne declared.

"It is not!"

"Is too!"

Mary laughed as they argued. Soon they were confiding the woes of growing up in a small community where most of the boys were their cousins.

"And they are such snitches," Pam wailed. "They tell on us if we do the least thing."

"Like skipping school three days in a row to attend the county fair and flirt with the cowboys," Jonah stated, coming in with a monstrous stack of fry bread and another huge bowl containing chips of various colors made from yams and other root vegetables.

Several aunts also entered bearing containers of food. The centerpiece arrived via one of the uncles and Trek Lanigan. When they removed the foil covering the baking pan, the delicious aroma of barbecued pork filled the air.

"Uncle Reno is expert at this," Trek told her, gesturing toward the meat. "He smokes the pork with mesquite chips and bastes it with a special sauce. Maybe you can get him to share the recipe. He won't give it to the rest of us."

Mary's stomach rumbled loudly.

Jonah shot her a teasing glance. "We'd better feed her before she starts biting."

After placing his grandfather first, then his mother, Jonah pulled her into line and stood protectively behind her when the cousins complained.

"Age has its privileges," Jonah declared and handed Mary a plate and took one for himself.

When her plate was loaded, at the urging of Jonah to "try this, take some of that," Mary wasn't sure where to go.

"This way," he said and led the way into the great room. He sat on a sofa that faced his grandfather and mother across the coffee table. "Here," he said, indicating Mary should sit beside him.

As the others returned, the older people filled the chairs while the younger ones settled on the floor. Feeling awkward among the chattering, friendly relatives, Mary decided to eat quickly and escape to her room. Or maybe she should go to the kitchen and start cleaning up in there.

Listening to the avid conversations, which included much teasing of the grandfather about his age, she surprised herself by eating every bite on her plate. Several others had finished, too, so she collected plates and carried them to the kitchen. Jonah followed with a load.

"Don't clean up," he ordered. "I've already promised to pay Pam and Julianne to do it. They like to earn extra cash."

Put that way, she could hardly continue. She stacked the dishes in the sink. "That was very good," she said. "Thank you for inviting me to join your family. I think I'll head upstairs now."

He shook his head. "You can't. Grandfather would be troubled if anyone left before the cake is cut. It's considered bad luck for the birthday person, you know."

Actually she didn't, and she wasn't sure whether he was putting her on or not.

He removed the cover from a sheet cake. Nine fat white candles were clustered together with a smaller one offset an inch or so from them. "My grandfather is ninety-one."

"He doesn't look it," Mary said sincerely.

"We age well."

Jonah gave her a sexy oblique glance that started her heart thumping. Yearning coursed through her, taking her by storm before she could put up barriers. She stood there, unable to think of anything to say.

"Help me light the candles," he requested.

The job was quickly done, then Jonah asked her to grab one end of the tray. They carried the cake to the great room.

Someone turned off the lights as soon as they appeared and started singing the birthday song. Mary listened to Jonah's fine baritone and picked out Pam's and Julianne's soprano voices.

Together she and Jonah placed the cake on the coffee table. His grandfather leaned forward and admired it while the song was finished.

"Make a wish!" the crowd called.

The old man thought for a moment, then blew out the candles in one breath. She laughed and applauded with the rest, then cut the cake at Jonah's urging. The girls brought in plates, Mary put squares of yellow butter cake on them and Jonah served the adults while the girls passed slices to the boy cousins. The two babies slept peacefully in adaptable car seats through the whole of the festivities.

Jonah's mother and aunts engaged Mary in a discussion of culinary skills. Apparently Jonah had told them she was a great cook. They discussed recipes and spices. It was a while before she realized the older women were expert at drawing out a person's life experiences.

Oddly she didn't mind sharing with them for they shared, too. One aunt and her two brothers had been in foster homes before the grandfather had learned of their plight and come for them and taken them home. Mary learned the three were not blood relatives, but part of the same tribe and so were honorary kin.

By the time everyone left, it was midnight. Mary checked the clock in amazement.

She looked around the great room, then went to the kitchen. There wasn't a plate to wash or spoon to put away. The dining room had been restored to its usual order. With nothing left to be done, she started for the stairs.

It didn't seem possible that it had been

hours since she'd tried to sneak past Jonah and go to her room.

He came inside and locked the door. Catching sight of her in the hallway, he smiled. "You were a hit with the folks."

"They were very nice."

He turned out the lamps so that only the hall sconces softly lit the area. They both moved forward. She stopped with a hand on the newel post, but didn't take the first step. She couldn't. Jonah blocked the way.

"Thanks for talking to the two girls. The rest of the cousins are boys, so they feel isolated sometimes."

"They were fun." She stood there in awkward silence, wishing she could think of something witty and entertaining, something that would entice him the way other women were able to do. Nothing came to mind.

His gaze roamed her face. His eyes seemed to darken. He lifted one hand and caressed her cheek. A tremor shook her.

He exhaled in a sigh. "Go to bed, cowgirl. You're tired and my control is slipping badly by the minute."

"What?" she said blankly.

He leaned closer. Her lips tingled. She realized she was waiting for his kiss. He realized it, too.

Humiliated by the aching hunger, she tried to push past him before she embarrassed herself more.

He caught her by the shoulders. "Don't you think it's the same for me?" he questioned softly. "I've never wanted a woman the way I want you."

"Why?"

"Because," he whispered, his breath touching her lips as he moved even closer. He shuddered, seemed to collect himself and stepped away. "Good night."

She raced up the stairs without looking back.

Chapter Five

Friday of the following week, Mary reviewed the livestock while waiting for Jonah to get off the phone. She'd gotten up early to exercise Attila, then get the ranch chores done.

Yesterday she'd worked with the cattle from dawn until dark, checking them for lost tags, pink eye, sores and other illnesses, then making a final count of the calves that would be trucked out on Saturday.

Now she was showered and dressed in clean clothing and, she admitted, rather excited. Today they were going to Lost Valley, Population 1,000…if one counted the dogs and cats, she assumed.

"Mary!"

Turning, she spotted Jonah at the back door. She hurried up the path to the lodge. Since the birthday party the previous Saturday, he had maintained the line between boss and wrangler. That suited her just fine.

"Would you make a list of items that we're running short of in the grocery?" he asked. "If there's only one or two left, then we'll need to get more."

She nodded and followed his tall, masculine form down the hall, conscious of his powerful stride and graceful way of moving. He was incredibly handsome in polished boots and jeans. His thighs were muscular, his hips and waist lean. He wore a white shirt with the cuffs rolled up on his forearms.

His body would be hard, his touch easy, if he kissed her again, if they came together in passion.

Annoyed with her wayward thoughts, she crossed the great room, then grabbed a notepad and pen from the store counter and started down the first row of shelves. The job didn't take long since the entire store was maybe ten feet by twelve, with a double row of shelves running down the middle and freezers and refrigerated cases lined up along the back wall.

A gum and candy display stood next to the

short counter. A central drawer located under the counter was lockable and had a money tray in it. The tray was empty.

Jonah kept an old cigar box on the counter. She peeked inside. It held a five-dollar bill, a few ones and quite a bit of loose change. She rolled her eyes. For a former big city ad executive, he certainly ran a loose ship, so to speak.

One thing she noticed—there were no tobacco or alcohol products on the premises.

"About ready?"

She glanced at Jonah, then back at her list. "Yes. Do you want to get more mosquito spray? There are two cans left."

"No. Bug season is over. We'll need chemical toe warmers and lip balm next month when the hunters arrive."

"Uh, are you expecting many?"

"The lodge will be full until the middle of December, when the hunting season is over. Then we get a break until the back country snow crowd arrives."

She handed over her list and headed to the ranch pickup when he indicated she should precede him outside. Once buckled up and on their way, she asked, "Do you need my room?"

"No." He glanced at her, his eyes dark, almost moody. "I was going to move upstairs when cold weather came, but the sunroom will do."

"It has a lot of windows," she said. "They aren't double panes like the rest of the lodge?"

"Not yet. We're putting our efforts in things that make money at the present, such as the guest rooms. Our clients prefer to dress without having a breeze on their backside. I'll add another blanket to the bed when the north wind blows." He chuckled.

Mary thought of the out-of-shape dudes who'd been on the paramilitary outing and their delight at returning to the cozy lodge. "The men enjoyed roughing it in the wilds."

"Yes. It was an accomplishment for them. They saw themselves as mountain men, one with nature and all that."

She gazed at the far peaks. Seemingly endless lines of mountains surrounded the valley and its little settlement.

"I feel like that here, too," she said. "It's different from the rodeo and racetrack. Those are held in cities. Here, you're actually close to nature." She thought of the tick. "Maybe too close," she added wryly.

"A lot of people would find it lonely, frightening in its vastness. People get lost every year."

"Are they found?"

He flashed her a sardonic glance. "Well, most of 'em."

She laughed. When he joined in, she found she liked the sound of his deeper tone blending with her higher, feminine voice, as if their laughter harmonized.

Falling silent, she observed the landscape with its hills and rocky outcroppings, the sage along the road and beyond that, the trees that marched upward in stately arrays.

The sense of isolation appealed to her. They hadn't passed another vehicle on the road. Other than fences, there wasn't a sign of human habitation. A person could breathe here, could relax and take life as it came.

Except for the nervousness induced by the man beside her and the occasional sense of danger that troubled her.

"Why the heavy sigh?" Jonah asked.

"It's peaceful here," she replied truthfully.

"You're more comfortable not having people around."

She tensed. He saw too much, this lean wolf of a man who'd chosen the wilds over civilization. "Nature is easier to deal with," she said lightly.

"Sometimes it can be treacherous, too. Sometimes it can sweep down and engulf you, the way a sudden storm comes over the mountains and drenches you in cold rain before you have time to get to shelter."

Like them, she thought. Like the way they reacted to each other—suddenly and taken unawares. Like a fire dancing all around them, the passion could erupt without warning. She'd never experienced desire like this. She wondered if he had.

Of course he had. He'd lived in New York, city of beautiful models and sophisticated women. Glancing at her own jeans-clad legs, she unconsciously sighed. She'd never wanted to be glamorous before. Not that she did now, but—

She cut off the rest of that thought.

His eyes met hers when he stopped at the

paved road that led into the town, controlled hunger in those smoky depths. She looked away with an effort, her heartbeat becoming irregular and too fast.

In town, he parked at a grocery and they went inside. He introduced her to the manager, who was working the cash register, spoke to a couple of other people, then grabbed a basket for their supplies. Going over the list she'd made, he told her why he was or wasn't replacing certain items.

"Without campers, we won't need cooking staples," he explained. "The hunters will have to be fed, but we rely on soup, chili and sandwiches, plus a hearty breakfast, to get us through the season. Get extra crackers in different varieties. They're popular as snacks as well as with the meals."

She nodded, taking the info in and adding it to her growing bank of knowledge on the ranch and its operations.

He touched her forehead, startling her. "Easy," he murmured. "Don't be so intense. You don't have to learn everything in one day." He paused, then added, "We don't have to take everything seriously."

She backed up a step. "I'm trying to impress my boss with my efficiency," she said in mocking tones.

Jonah gave an amused snort. "Believe me, I'm impressed."

Her blood warmed at the implied praise. She could grow used to him and his easy ways.

The heaviness returned to her spirits. She wouldn't be here long enough to get used to anything. She would do her job then move on. But there was something about the ranch and/or the mountains that pulled at her heart-strings.

Or maybe it was just her boss.

After they toured the farmer's market, buying what seemed to her to be a ton of vegetables and fruits, they stored everything in coolers under a tarp in the pickup.

"Lunch," he said, backing out of the parking space.

He drove them to a lodge beside the lake, which was a reservoir supplying the town's water. "The Daltons own the lodge. They did most of the building on it. The logs came from their place." He pointed to the massive pillars that supported the roof when they entered the lobby. "This way."

In the dining room, they were seated beside a window so they could see the water. An RV resort was on the opposite shore. Less than half the camping spaces were occupied, but the place had probably been full last weekend.

Another sign of the changing seasons, she mused.

A walking path ran around the lake and across the dam located at the narrow end of the reservoir. The lodge and the town were named after the area, Lost Valley. It looked like a paradise to her.

From an adjoining room came the sounds of laughter and happy voices. She smiled at their merriment and relaxed.

Jonah removed his hat and laid the dark gray Stetson in the chair next to him. He took care of his sunglasses by sticking the ear piece in a buttonhole.

Mary hesitated, then did the same. She'd braided her hair into one fat plait that lay along her back, so it was confined.

"That's better," her boss said in satisfaction. "Although it's a shame to confine all that hair in a braid."

"It gets in the way if I don't."

He continued gazing at her until she glared at him, then he smiled slightly and turned his eyes toward the waitress who stopped beside the table. "What's happening?" he asked, nodding toward the adjoining room.

The door was partially closed, so they couldn't see the party going on inside.

"Wedding celebration," she said and gave a moue of disappointment. "The last Dalton bit the dust over the holiday. The wedding was out of state, so they're having a belated family celebration here."

Jonah nodded. "Yeah, Trevor got hitched to some gal he met in Texas."

The waitress, who was maybe twenty, frowned. "They all married outsiders except for Seth. He at least married someone who lived here in town."

Mary sympathized with the local women who hadn't been chosen by the apparently very desirable Dalton bachelors. "How many Daltons are there?" she asked.

"Six," the waitress said. "Five guys, one

girl. They were all orphans taken in by their uncle, Nicholas Dalton."

"With the uncle, that makes seven," Jonah said.

Seven Daltons, seven devils. An odd sensation, like icy water, ran over Mary's scalp. For a second she felt disoriented, as if the ground were shifting under her, as if she were suddenly in another time, another place...

Tinkerbell, Tinkerbell, got in trouble and went to jail.

Startled, Mary sat perfectly still, listening to voices she knew were only in her head. When she'd first been sent to the children's ranch, she'd heard the taunt often, but gradually it faded from memory. Until now. The childish singsong echoed through her skull as it had in the distant past, hurting in some way she couldn't describe. She felt confused, as if she were in the head of another person, a child intent on holding her own against the older children.

It was strange and disorienting, almost scary. Yet the child wasn't afraid. Mary knew that, but she didn't know how she knew.

"Mary? Are you okay?"

She stared at Jonah, then realized he was asking about her. Slowly she lowered her hands, which she'd clasped over her ears as if to block out the youthful mocking voices.

"Yes. I'm fine." She quickly gave her order to the young waitress, then stared at the smooth water of the lake, which mirrored the perfect blue of the sky.

Tinkerbell, Tinkerbell...

The taunt seemed like a memory, but it wasn't. She knew it wasn't—she remembered every detail of her life in the orphanage—yet there was some fragment of realism to it. She didn't know why. Or why it was so upsetting.

"Are you sure you feel okay?"

Jonah was looking at her, concern in the penetrating gray-blue gaze. The waitress was gone, so he must have given his order, but she hadn't heard it. She'd been too lost in…in…a dream? A memory? An hallucination?

"I'm fine," she insisted. Clasping her hands tightly in her lap, she hoped this was true. She felt as if she just might be going insane.

Composing herself, she focused on asking her boss about the ranch and his plans for its future. He spoke of building the small herd to several hundred, of perhaps adding a camp for inner-city youth in a few years.

"I'd like to research and write a book about how businesses can integrate community service work into their schedules and operations. By giving teenagers summer jobs or letting them fill in for their parents, the workers can get a break to make repairs on their home or something."

She was astonished at the ideas he had and asked several questions. When he confessed he'd written a book that had become a best seller five years ago, she couldn't believe it. "Well, you're versatile," she murmured, feeling more than a little daunted by his brilliance.

"So are you." He spoke on a quiet note, introspective in his manner. "You can cook, tend cattle, train horses and plan for the Olympics."

The sincerity in his manner almost got her choked up. She managed a smile and waved aside her accomplishments. They were nothing compared to his.

"Some people don't recognize their own talents," he said with a mock-scolding frown.

She suddenly felt brilliant and beautiful and as poised as a queen. "Well, we know our limitations."

Their food arrived, and Mary found it delicious, with surprising gourmet touches in the sun-dried tomatoes served with the trout and blueberries sprinkled in the spinach salad seasoned with balsamic vinegar and warm honey.

Jonah continued telling her of his plans for the future. "The problem," he concluded when the waitress had removed their empty dishes, "is getting reliable help, especially with a youth camping program."

"College kids often need summer jobs," she said.

"Uh, I don't think so."

Mary studied the rueful expression that accompanied the words. "Is there a story behind this refusal?"

He sighed, then admitted, "I tried a college girl earlier in the year. It didn't work out."

"She developed an interest in you."

His grimace was enough to tell her this was true.

She shrugged. "You're a handsome man.

Working together breeds an intimacy of sorts, I suppose."

"Does it usually do that for you?"

Startled, her gaze flew to his. "No, of course not," she told him. Except for those few moments between them, honesty compelled her to add, but she didn't say it aloud. "I avoid entanglements of any sort," she said, her manner brusque and prudish.

"I was afraid of that."

Again their eyes met. She studied him, not sure she was reading him correctly.

"There's an attraction between us, cowgirl. Are we going to pretend there isn't, that the kiss never happened?" His manner was wry, as if he laughed at both of them and the puzzling threads of interest that arced between them.

"Yes. As you said, we don't have to act on an impulse." She sounded breathless, more as if she questioned him rather than denied the possibility of something between them.

But an undercurrent of emotion hummed through her veins, filling her with the odd longing she'd experienced of late.

"Maybe," he murmured, an assessing light

in the smoky blue eyes that observed her so solemnly.

"I don't get mixed up with my boss."

"Or anyone."

She met his gaze levelly.

His dark eyebrows rose slightly. "There was someone. Once. Wasn't there?" he demanded when she was silent.

"A long time ago. When I was very young and much too trusting."

"What happened?"

"He was engaged. He didn't think that it should interfere with our relationship."

"Ouch," Jonah said.

She smiled. "Yeah, it hurt. But it was a good lesson."

"You learned not to trust men."

"Handsome, laughing men," she amended.

"You said I was handsome. This must be one of those 'damned with faint praise' moments."

He was teasing her, and it felt odd. There was an attraction, and that was weird. He made her laugh, and that was the scariest thing of all.

"Excuse me," she murmured and rose.

She found the restroom and hid in there for several minutes until she had all the strange emotions and quivers under control once more. Jonah was just a man—a handsome, intelligent one, but just a man—and she'd learned never, never, never to trust the attraction of the moment.

Crossing the lobby on her return to the restaurant, Mary was nearly run down by a mob of laughing people. A man crashed into her, knocking her off balance.

She grabbed his shirt front and they both nearly went down. "I'm sorry," she murmured automatically.

"It was my fault. I didn't see you," he said. He took hold of her upper arms until they were steady on their feet.

She gazed up into eyes as blue as her own. His dark eyebrows were sprinkled with gray while the thick shock of hair that tumbled over his forehead was totally silver. He had a hint of a cleft in his chin. She smiled politely and tried to pull away.

His hands tightened suddenly, harshly on her arms. Startled, she reacted instinctively, thrusting him away with her hands on his chest. Immediately he released her and collapsed onto the red and black Native American rug covering the oak floor.

"Sir?" she said, worried by the pallor in his face and the way his hand went to his chest. "Sir?" She knelt beside him, not sure what was wrong.

"Let me see him," a male voice ordered. "I'm a doctor."

She moved to the old man's head while a young man, with blue eyes identical to those of the nearly unconscious man, bent over him. A woman, also gray-haired, dropped to her knees and took one limp hand in hers and held it to her cheek.

The man's wife, Mary presumed.

A lovely redhead pushed through the group and knelt on Mary's other side. "I have the medical kit," she said. She opened a black bag, removed a blood pressure cuff and handed it to the doctor. "What happened?" she asked Mary.

"We bumped into each other, then I...I don't know exactly what happened. Except he clutched his chest and couldn't seem to breathe."

Strong hands lifted her and set her aside as if she weighed no more than a child. "He's had a couple of spells with his heart," another dark-haired, blue-eyed man told her, his manner worried but his tone kind.

"Uncle Nick?" the doctor said. "We're going to the clinic." He glanced around at the others. "As soon as we get him stabilized, we'll airlift him into Boise."

"Is it his heart?" the older woman asked.

The doctor shrugged slightly. "He has a rapid pulse, but the heartbeat is strong and even. It's more as if he's had a shock or something." He frowned as if puzzled.

"Could it be a stroke?" a petite, dark-haired woman asked, pushing past the others. She clutched the arm of the tall man beside her.

Mary found herself at the back of the group. She'd already realized this must be the infamous Dalton clan that lived on the ranch next to Jonah's place. The men were so tall she couldn't see what was happening to their uncle.

They also had lean, sinewy frames and the sky-blue eyes of the older man, she noted. Their hair was still the rich brown-black color appropriate to their age, which she judged to be in the late twenties and early thirties. A couple of them had the stubborn wave that fell across their forehead the same as the eldest Dalton.

A hand settled on her shoulder. "Ready to go? There's nothing we can do here," Jonah said, his gaze raking over her face as if he knew what she'd done.

"I didn't mean to hurt him," she said, automatically going on the defensive. "He was holding on to me. I sh-shoved him. I only wanted to get away. I didn't mean to hurt him," she repeated.

"I know. I saw the whole thing. It was an accident."

His words eased a bit of the anxiety. "We can't just leave, not until I know he's going to be all right."

"I'll check with Beau later. He's the doctor."

Jonah guided her outside to the truck and helped her in as if she were an invalid. Her fingers trembled when she fastened the seat belt. She couldn't make them stop. Slipping on the sunglasses didn't feel more secure, either, she found. Her world seemed chaotic and uncertain, as if she'd done a terrible thing when she'd reacted without thinking.

"You okay?" he asked when he was buckled in and ready to go, his hand on the key.

"Yes." She managed a smile. "I've never had quite that effect on a man before."

"He'll be okay. Uncle Nick is as strong as a bull moose and twice as stubborn."

"Oh, well, that takes a load off my mind."

His soft laughter did, oddly, ease her worry. He started the engine and drove out of the parking lot and onto the road that would take them home. She glanced back in time to see the Daltons come out of the lodge. The older man was walking, a nephew on either side of him, ready to grab him if he faltered.

A caring, protective family.

For the briefest moment, she felt the soul-deep yearning for a family she couldn't remember and had probably never had.

But sometimes they seemed so real to her, a sort of waking memory when she got up on some mornings, as if she'd been with them in her dreams, running through green fields, laughing and happy and carefree…

"He seems to be better," she told Jonah, shrugging off the longing and the loneliness it induced. "He's walking on his own."

"Good."

On the trip, she recounted the incident to herself several times. One minute all had been fine, then they'd glanced at each other, their faces no more than a foot apart as they steadied, and something had happened.

She couldn't figure out what.

It was as if a hand had grabbed him by the throat and choked him. Emotion had flashed across his face. A sort of agony, she thought. Well, he must have been in pain. A heart attack could happen with a sudden, terrible pain, couldn't it?

Or a stroke?

A shock, the doctor had said.

He'd looked into her face and been shocked?

"Still beating yourself up?" Jonah asked shortly before they arrived home.

"Still worrying. How old is Mr. Dalton?"

"Early seventies, I would think."

She sighed and worried some more.

He glanced at her thoughtfully. "You know,

it seemed to me the trouble started when he saw your face up close. Those eyes…" He let the thought trail off as he pulled to a stop in front of the lodge and cut the engine.

"Mine or his?"

Leaning across the seat, he pulled her shades down her nose enough so he could gaze into her eyes. She anxiously waited for his judgment.

"Yours," he said in a soft, husky voice.

The thoughtful frown disappeared as he continued to gaze at her. Her heart upped its tempo. She swallowed nervously. When his lips parted slightly, her own did, too, without her conscious command.

He wanted to kiss her. She wanted it, too, so much it sent frissons of panic spiraling through her.

"This isn't good," she murmured, more to herself than him. She knew not to let herself become involved with anyone, for any reason.

He shook his head, muttered under his breath, then got out of the truck and started unloading groceries onto the porch.

But not before she'd seen the heat in the cool depths of his eyes. Not before an arc of lightning flashed between them. Not before an answering warmth echoed in her, matching the fire in him.

She jumped down from the pickup and helped with the chores. After getting the groceries inside, he put her to work stocking the tiny store while he proceeded to the kitchen.

When she finished, she hurried down the hall. "What about my eyes?" she demanded, letting the irritation show.

He leaned against the counter by the sink and studied her again. "Remove the shades."

She did so, uncomfortable with his scrutiny.

"The resemblance is uncanny," he murmured. "I didn't realize how strong it was until I saw you with the whole gang of Daltons."

"Blue eyes and dark hair don't indicate a bond of blood," she said, scoffing at his words.

"It's more than coloring. You're tall. Like the Daltons. And as leggy as a new calf. Like the Daltons. You have fair skin. Like the Daltons. And a slight cleft in the chin."

"So?"

"So a long time ago Nick Dalton's wife was killed in a car accident. His three-year-old daughter disappeared from the crash site. She was never seen again. I was around ten at the time and remember the reporters and TV camera crews swarming the county, asking everyone questions."

Mary's scoffing attitude disappeared. "How terrible."

"Yeah. Uncle Nick has been looking for her ever since. I wonder if he thought you could be the missing child. I think she'd be about your age by now."

Mary recalled the old man's expression when he'd peered into her face. He'd opened his mouth as if to say something, then had clutched his chest. "If he thought only for a second I could be his lost daughter, it would be an awful shock."

Jonah looked deep into her eyes.

"Yeah, that's what I think happened."

Chapter Six

Jonah tasted the stew, wondered what to add, then replaced the lid. Mary could fix it when she came to the house. He glanced out the window and saw her checking her stallion's leg. She'd already looked over the cattle and the cowponies and opened the gate to the next pasture so the herd could move there to graze. She was very conscientious about doing the ranch work first.

His blood stirred again. She didn't seem to realize she was a very attractive woman. Unfortunately he did.

He liked her long, lean build. The vision of those legs wrapped around him haunted his dreams and his waking hours at odd moments. Like now.

Shifting his jeans, he eased some of the tension caused by the hardening of his body.

He couldn't look away as she removed her gloves and stuffed them in a back pocket, then perched on the fence while she perused the land and the mountains that guarded it.

Her fingers, he'd noticed, were long and slender like the rest of her, her hands narrow, almost delicate, but she could do as much work as any wrangler he'd ever known.

She'd been upset after the happening at lunch, but she seemed calm now. Strange, that incident. He felt there was something, a clue of some kind, that hovered just beyond his consciousness, a hint that he should grab and examine more closely. Nothing came to mind.

Thinking there was a connection between his new wrangler and the Daltons was probably stupid. Just because she looked exactly like them didn't have to mean anything. Everyone was said to have a twin somewhere in the world.

But her resemblance to them was uncanny. He studied her again—the nearly black hair, the slender height and the eyes, those to-die-for eyes. But then, one of the Dalton wives had eyes nearly the same shade of blue.

Ease up, he advised his circling thoughts. Before she left, he would know the truth. Or else.

The stallion pushed his muzzle into her lap. She scratched his ears as demanded.

Jonah smiled. She loved the old flea-bag, but that love had come at a hefty price. She'd sunk her fortune and her future into the jumper.

Just as he'd done here at the ranch.

For a second, he felt that bond between them, a golden thread of hopes and plans and dogged determination. Yeah, he could identify with that.

Man, next thing he knew he'd be all misty-eyed and choked up. Snorting in mock amusement, he went to the door.

"Dinner," he called.

She turned and waved, smoothed Attila's forelock between her fingers, then lightly jumped to the ground.

The phone rang in the office at that moment. He went to answer. "Towbridge Ranch."

"Uh, Jonah, this is Zack Dalton."

"Hey, Zack," he said. He had a feeling he knew what was coming.

"I have a couple of questions about that gal in the restaurant with you today," Zack said.

"The new wrangler," Jonah acknowledged. "I thought you might be interested in her."

"Right. She nearly gave Uncle Nick a heart attack."

"How is he?"

"Okay, I think. Beau gave him something, so he's sleeping right now. I thought this would be a good time to check things out. Keith said her name is Mary McHale?"

"That's right. She saw the Help Wanted sign I posted in the Trading Post. I interviewed her by phone and hired her on the spot. She's been here almost two weeks."

"How old is she?"

"Twenty-six, she says."

Zack was quiet for a minute. "Tink would have been twenty-seven in September."

"Was that your uncle's daughter? Her name was Tink?" Jonah asked.

"A nickname. Her real name was Theresa Ann. She's been missing since she was three and a half years old."

"I heard the story. Mary's birthday is in

March. She gave Wyoming as her place of birth. That's where she grew up."

There was a moment of silence. Jonah heard Mary enter through the back and caught a glimpse of her heading up the stairs. His heart gave a funny little hitch.

"Well," Zack said, "I guess that settles it. I didn't really think she could be the long missing child, but I had to call. Uncle Nick is convinced she could be. I'll tell him she isn't."

"Wait a minute," Jonah said, lowering his voice. "This is probably nothing, but Mary was raised in an orphanage."

"Where?"

"Wyoming."

"Do you know anything about her family?"

"Not much. She was abandoned by her father and lived with some old woman who took her in until the cops picked her up. Apparently the officials decided she was five years old."

"My God," Zack muttered.

"Yeah. Her past is open to speculation."

"I've got to question her. I'll be right over."

"Give us a couple of hours. We haven't eaten yet. She's in the shower now."

He could hear the water running. During the week, he'd noticed she liked to clean up before eating. After the meal, she went to her room. He had no idea what she did during that time. Her light was usually out around nine.

"Okay, we'll see you—"

"Don't bring the whole gang," Jonah warned. "You'll scare the hell out of her."

"Right. I'll shoot the others unless they agree to stay here. Seth will come with me."

"Should I warn her or let your visit be a surprise?" Jonah asked wryly, knowing the whole bunch might show up in spite of Zack's efforts.

"Whatever works for you. See you around eight then?"

"Yeah, sure."

Jonah hung up and returned to the kitchen. Mary arrived a couple of minutes later. As with everything she did, she was quick and efficient in the bath. He quickly forced that image out of his mind.

"Taste this," he said, holding a spoonful of stew toward her.

She did. "Shall I fix it?"

"Be my guest."

Nodding in her solemn way, she added spices and a small amount of sugar. He took note of the additions. She stirred the stew, tasted, then held the spoon out to him.

"Perfect," he declared after closing his hand over hers to steady the spoon while he took a bite. She was still upset over the incident in town, he decided.

When she turned from him to fill their bowls, he had to resist an urge to run his fingers through her hair and remove the ribbon at the back of her neck to let it flow free. The thick hank fell to her waist. He could imagine the way it would cascade around a man as she bent over him and they made love for hour after lovely hour.

"Damn," he said, but under his breath so she didn't hear. He grabbed his food and followed her into the dining room.

While they ate, he noticed her eyes stayed on the view of the mountains, which were highlighted by the deepening colors of the sunset. A faraway look permeated the azure depths. He was pleased that she'd left the shades in her room.

A sign that she trusted him?

His libido had started humming even stronger the moment she'd appeared in her sweat suit, smelling sweetly of shampoo and powder, her hair tied loosely at the back of her neck. His heart had performed its little lunging act.

Perhaps he'd better warn her not to be too trusting of him. His control slipped a cog whenever she was near.

One thing he didn't need was an added complication in his life. Neither did she. He sighed and set his mind on other matters, such as the pending Dalton visit.

"We may have company this evening," he said.

Her eyes cut to him, wariness immediately visible.

"A couple of the Daltons want to talk to you."

"Because of what happened?"

"Partly. They, uh, want to ask you a couple of questions, I think."

She gave him a wary glance. "What about?"

"We'll have to wait until they arrive to find out." He ignored her frown and downed the rest of the delicious dinner, sure that her feminine curiosity would keep her downstairs for the evening.

"Is it about their missing cousin?" she asked, suspicious.

Jonah nodded. "You're quick on the uptake."

She slammed her hand on the table. "I'm not their uncle's long-lost daughter. I remember my father."

"You said you were three, maybe four, when you were abandoned. Did you ever see him again?"

She met his eyes without flinching. Without emotion, she said, "No. He left me outside a bar one night. Some man was threatening him with a gun, so he drove off. He never came back."

"Honey, I'm sorry," Jonah said, not planning the words. They just came up from someplace deep inside. He tried to take her hand, but she pulled away.

"I'm fine. I don't need your pity."

"I know," he said, "but maybe that child does."

She turned stubbornly back to her food and left the room as soon as she finished eating.

MARY HAD LEFT her bedroom door ajar, so she heard the footsteps on the wooden porch, then the baritone of male voices when the men came inside. Jonah, helping someone in the store, called out a greeting.

Her heart thudded with the dull, wordless fear that children experience when dealing with a world beyond their control. She'd once known that world well.

Standing, she squared her shoulders, resisted the urge to put on the tinted glasses, and headed downstairs.

"Ah, here she is," Jonah said, smiling as if this were a social call. "Mary, this is Zack Dalton, the assistant sheriff of the county, and his cousin, Seth Dalton, an attorney in Lost Valley."

"How do you do?" she said politely. That's all she had to do—be polite, hear them out, keep her distance.

"Good evening," Seth, who had dark eyes, spoke to her. "Thanks for agreeing to see us."

"Yes," the lawman said. "This is probably

a false alarm, but we have to check it out, you understand?"

She nodded.

Jonah motioned toward the hall. "Let's go into the dining room. I've put on a fresh pot of coffee."

Mary let herself be herded down the corridor and into the pleasant dining room. She glanced at the mountains silhouetted against the twilight skyline and felt uneasy. Jonah brought in coffee and settled at the table with the other three.

Silence prevailed while they flavored and tasted the hot brew. Mary warmed her hands around the mug before taking a sip. She forced herself into absolute stillness in a place where nothing could touch or hurt her.

The Dalton men glanced at each other. Zack nodded slightly, apparently a signal for the other man to begin.

"Our uncle, Nicholas Dalton, once had a wife and daughter. Aunt Milly was killed in a car wreck, but the child, who was three and a half at the time, disappeared. Her name was Theresa Ann Dalton," Seth ended.

Tinkerbell, Tinkerbell, got in trouble and...

Mary's hands jerked, sloshing coffee over the rim of the cup as the childhood taunt echoed in her head. She quickly wiped the spill and placed a napkin under the cup. She clasped her trembling hands in her lap so they couldn't see.

Seth's eyes narrowed. "Do you recognize the name?"

Mary shook her head.

He continued the story. "The detectives found a man's boot prints and the imprint of a child's sneaker in the dust beside the road where the accident happened. Our cousin was never seen again."

"I'm sorry," Mary said. "It must have been horrible for your uncle."

"Yes. It's been over twenty-three years. He's never given up hope." Seth cleared his throat. "Jonah said you were raised in an orphanage?"

She'd been expecting the question. "Yes. In Wyoming."

"Would you mind telling us about yourself?" the attorney requested, his manner gentle.

She realized she would have to tell them

everything to satisfy their concerns. Taking a calming breath and reaching into the vast stillness she'd learned to summon when she needed it, she began, first telling them about coming out of the ladies' room at a bar one night and finding the man she thought was her father facing a gun. She'd hidden behind a garbage can and waited to see what happened.

"You never saw him again after he left?" Seth asked.

"That's right. I waited for two days, but he never came back. The bartender found me on the second day. He gave me food and let me wash up in the restroom. When I heard him telling the waitress that he was going to call the police and report me, I was scared. I thought that meant they would lock me up, so I ran away."

"How old were you?"

"Well, I remembered being three, but the police and orphanage people figured I was five when I was picked up. My father and I traveled around a lot before the bar incident. I recall living on a ranch where he worked one summer and fall, then we went to a warm place, then came north again. It was late March when he left me, according to the bartender, and early March when the police picked me up."

"You were on your own for nearly a year? How?" Zack asked, taking over the interrogation. "How could a child your age care for herself?"

"An old woman took me under her wing. Her name was Mary. I stayed at her house. A boy named Jimmy was her neighbor. He found me and took me to her. He helped Mary take me to the county health department for my shots and some medicine once when I had a cold. He died of an overdose."

A large hand covered hers in her lap. She glanced at Jonah, then down at their hands. She blinked the sudden tears away. "I'm okay."

"I know," he said in his wonderfully quiet, soothing way. He gave her clasped hands a squeeze, then released her.

She took a breath, then finished the tale. "The orphanage decided I was five. I said my name was Mary since I couldn't recall my real name. At Mary's, everyone called me 'kid.' The orphanage director added the

McHale since they were at the M's in naming abandoned babies anyway. They gave me a birthday and a birth certificate."

"You've had a hard life," Seth said with compassion. "I'm sorry we had to make you bring it up again."

She unclasped her hands and picked up the mug. She even managed a smile. "It's okay. The memories don't hurt, not really. I have the life I want, so I'm—" she had to pause so she wouldn't stumble over the word "—happy now," she finished.

"You don't remember ever living in Idaho?" Zack asked.

"I don't. I'm sorry. Your cousin would be a lucky girl to have you as a family, but I'm not her. I remember my father."

"The man who drove off and left a child to fend for herself," Jonah muttered in disgust.

The Dalton men glanced at each other. Apprehension flowed in a series of goose bumps along Mary's arms.

Seth asked, "You don't recall your mother or anything before you were abandoned?"

Mary shook her head. "It's a total blank."

She'd often thought it was odd that she

couldn't. There were a few memories of traveling around the country, but it was as if her life had started at that moment in the tavern parking lot. She could recall everything since that instant.

Extreme fear, the psychologist who came to the orphanage once a month had declared. It could block memory or etch the scene deeply into the psyche forever.

Zack rubbed along the ridge of his nose, appearing deep in thought. The others waited.

At last he dropped his hand to the table. "There's one other thing."

"What?" Mary and Jonah said together.

"A scar." The lawman took a sip of coffee, then leaned toward her over the table. "Do you have any scars?"

"A cut on my knee where a horse kicked me once."

"That's it?"

"Yes."

He sighed deeply, his expression showing equal parts frustration and defeat. "Our cousin had a scar on her thigh, near her hip, where she fell on a broken bottle. It left three puncture wounds, like the points of a triangle."

Mary stared out at the night. The hills were darker shadows against a dark sky, blocking out the stars. The moon was a thin sliver hanging low in the sky. Like the night her father had left her.

"You have a tattoo," Jonah said.

A lightning stroke of shock flashed through her entire being. "How do you know that?" she demanded.

"I saw it when you were in the pool at the hot spring. I didn't want to frighten you, especially since I'd given you a gun, so I backed off, then called out at the edge of the woods so you would know I was a safe distance away."

She felt the heat fly to her face and knew twin spots of anger and embarrassment glowed like spotlights on her cheeks.

"I only saw you from the back," he quickly assured her, "and spotted what I thought was a unicorn tattoo on your leg. It was high up, near your hip. It is a tattoo, isn't it?"

"Yes. A friend who followed the rodeo circuit did it for me on my twenty-first birthday.

It was a symbol of freedom. As of that day I was of age no matter where I went or what I wanted to do."

"As long as it was within the law," Zack added wryly.

"Of course," Mary murmured, summoning an impish grin. "I'm a very law-abiding person."

The three men laughed.

A nice sound. They were nice people. Her eyes went to Jonah. He was, too. For a moment she was tempted to tell them she was the missing child and thus gain the benefits of a loving and apparently wealthy family.

Common sense prevailed. Her rule for making it through life was to be polite, be attentive, keep a distance.

Seth, the one she thought was the older of the two, sobered and gave her a searching look. "Would you be willing to visit Uncle Nick and talk to him?"

The question caught her off guard, causing a flurry of panic in her. "I don't know. Why would he want to see me?"

"That's a good idea," Zack told his cousin, then turned to her. "I think it would make

Uncle Nick feel better. It would ease his mind if he could talk to you personally and see for himself that you're not the one he wants so much for you to be."

"Right," Seth said. "Sunday would be good. How about coming over to the ranch for dinner around one? Then you and Uncle Nick can have a quiet talk while the rest of us do the dishes or something."

Mary observed the three men, all watching her and waiting for an answer. Dread robbed her of speech. She didn't know why the idea of meeting with the Dalton patriarch bothered her.

"I'll take you over," Jonah volunteered.

"Good." Seth rose as if all was settled. So did his cousin.

"Wait," she said.

The men paused, their eyes on her.

"I don't think that's necessary," she told them, sounding truculent instead of reasonable.

"Are you scared?" Jonah asked with unexpected insight.

"No, of course not. I don't want to upset Mr. Dalton again, that's all."

"You won't," Seth assured her. "Believe me, he'll come over here if you don't go over there."

The cousins nodded in unison, ending her argument.

"All right," she reluctantly agreed.

She stayed where she was while Jonah saw the other two out. When they were gone, she fled to her room with barely a "Good night" to her boss. She needed to be alone, to think.

Tinkerbell...Tinkerbell...

Curling up on the bed, she put her hands over her ears and squeezed her eyes shut. "I'm not. I'm not," she said to the laughing, clamoring voices inside her head.

But who was that child? And who were the children who teased her?

Chapter Seven

Mary looked over her clothes with a critical eye at noon on Sunday. Since she didn't have much formal wear, it didn't take her long to settle on navy-blue slacks with a blue-striped blouse. She pulled her hair into a ponytail, then twisted it into a loose knot and secured it with a couple of butterfly clips. After adding coral lipstick to combat the paleness of her face, she decided she was ready.

She had two purses, one beige, the other black. Selecting the beige to go with her beige flats, she stuffed her wallet, a tissue and the lipstick inside, then headed down the steps.

Actually she would be glad to get away from the house. Yesterday the cattle truck had carted away the calves that had been sold. It was a necessary part of ranch operations, but the mama cows had been bawling for their babies since then, all afternoon and into the night, so that it had been difficult to get to sleep.

She'd been glad to see the sun come up that morning and had gotten out of bed even earlier than usual. While she was checking the water in the cattle trough, the cattle had crowded around her, mooing plaintively as if expecting her to resolve their concerns. She'd felt sorry for them and had said so at breakfast.

Her boss had assured her they would forget their little ones in a couple of days, then he'd gone back to eating the blueberry pancakes he'd prepared from a mix.

Maybe they would forget. Or maybe they just gave up, knowing it was useless to keep calling when the calves didn't reappear after a few hours. Being prey to other animals surely must have given them instincts regarding death and disappearance as well as survival.

Hearing Jonah's voice, she paused at the last step and waited quietly for him to finish his business.

He was in the office, on the phone with someone who had a lot of questions about making a reservation. She noted he was wearing navy slacks with a white, long-sleeved shirt, cuffs rolled up as yesterday. No tie.

He hung up the phone. "Ready?"

"Yes."

"We'll go by the back road. It may be rougher than the county road, but it's shorter."

"Fine."

When they were in the truck, he said, "This isn't a death sentence."

She faced the road as he followed the circle of the drive. "I never thought it was." She paused. "I admit I'm nervous. I don't really have anything to say to Mr. Dalton."

"We'll play it by ear," Jonah told her.

As if he was on her side and would take her part against the others. She cast him a furtive glance as they took the road through the campground. Only two RVs remained.

The gravel lane led them to a one-lane bridge over a wide, shallow stream so clear she could see a fish idly waving its tail to hold it in place behind a rock.

"A trout," Jonah said, pointing toward the spot.

"I see it."

From there, the road wound steadily upward until they crested the hill, then it zigzagged down to a meadow, curved around a series of stony bluffs, then climbed again.

"You can see the roof of the ranch house where Keith and Janis live off to your right. It's at the base of those red-layered cliffs to the north. The cliffs and those three intersecting ridges form the boundaries of our ranch."

She peered over the landscape until she spotted a metal roof gleaming in the sun. "Yes, there it is."

Ahead of them, she noticed the land dipped and flattened out between two peaks, forming the rough shape of a saddle. The road they followed skirted the south side of the meadow, rose upward to the flat place between the hill tops, then disappeared on the other side.

At the top of the saddle, Jonah stopped and cut the engine. He hit the buttons that rolled down the windows.

The balsam scent of the forest wafted into the truck. Along with it came a freshness that she instinctively identified with water. From far away came the faint roar of the rushing river.

An acute sense of loneliness assailed her...

But she wasn't alone. Jonah sat silently beside her, his gaze on the land. She became aware of his warmth and the spicy aroma of his aftershave, his calm steady nature that seemed a part of the land and the mountains, as if he, like the granite ridges outlining the hills, had always been there and always would.

His breath touched her temple, stirring a few tendrils that had escaped her ponytail.

Yearning flowed through her, becoming a need to lean against him, to have him hold her, to keep her safe. No, no, she didn't need anyone. This meeting with the Dalton patriarch must be bothering her more than she realized. She would be okay. Really.

She followed his line of sight to the crags rising above the other mountains. Clouds pushed in from the western side but hadn't yet engulfed the mountains.

"Will there be a storm?" she asked, uneasiness spearing through her.

"Not likely. The clouds aren't thunderheads, although they could change as the day wears on." He moved back to his seat and buckled up. "We'd better get going."

Another ten minutes passed in silence as he navigated the gravel road, dodging a few rocks that had washed down from the steeper side and the potholes that lined one rough section.

Gazing ahead, she noticed that the road cut across a rather steep slope, forming a break through a thick growth of evergreen trees. Below them, the slope gentled into a lovely meadow, much wider than the earlier one.

Her heart plunged as if they had taken a sudden wrong turn and gone over a cliff. It started beating so hard she could hear it in her ears. Startled, she glanced at Jonah, then back at the land.

"We're on the Dalton ranch," he said.

"I know."

"Yeah? How?"

"I assumed, when we dropped over the saddle, we were on their place. That was the last high point where we could still see the red cliffs to find our way back."

He nodded. "I forgot how sharp you are. You always connect the dots."

"Well," she said with fake modesty, "I try."

"The first Dalton named his spread the Seven Devils Ranch," he continued. "He came west at the end of the Civil War to start a new life."

"And his own dynasty," she concluded when Jonah stopped talking.

"It certainly seems that way now. Uncle Nick and the orphans are a formidable bunch to cross, or so I've heard."

She pushed her sunglasses snugly against her nose.

"Hey, I didn't mean to scare you."

"I'm not scared." She clasped her hands in her lap and prayed for this to be true. "Why do you call him Uncle Nick?"

Jonah chuckled. "Everyone in the county does. It probably started with the six orphans, then all their friends joined in, then the rest of the locals. He prefers it. By the way, he re-married this summer. We call her Aunt Fay."

Mary inhaled slowly, deeply. "Just one big happy family, huh?"

"For now," he said on a more solemn note. "All families have their ups and downs."

They crested a final hill. She gasped as the home quarters of the Dalton place spread before them like a picture on a postcard— sprawling ranch house of logs, timber and stone, barns and stables, pastures with cows and horses, people greeting each other with hugs and slaps on the back.

It was too lovely to be real.

SETH DALTON WAS there to open the door as soon as the truck's wheels stopped turning. He took her elbow and helped her out. A pretty woman with red hair stood beside an old-fashioned horse rail similar to the one at Jonah's lodge. She smiled warmly at Mary.

"Mary, this is my wife, Amelia," Seth said.

"Hello." Amelia clasped Mary's hand between both of hers. "I didn't get a glimpse of you in all the excitement at the restaurant, but now I see what all the fuss was about. You do look remarkably like a Dalton, Mary."

"She's much quieter," Jonah said with just the right amount of wry humor in the words.

Seth and Amelia laughed in delight. "Come

inside," Amelia invited, still holding Mary's hand as if they were the best of friends. "Everyone is dying to meet you."

A knot lodged in Mary's throat as they went toward the rustic but attractive ranch house. The center part was constructed of logs, but the wings on either side were stone at the bottom and timber from the windows to the roof. A huge slab of granite formed the step to the front porch, anchoring the structure to the earth. From the open windows came the sound of cheerful voices intermingled in an intimate harmony.

It was a happy place, Mary mused. A safe, happy place.

For a second, the awful anguish of being left alone in the night threatened to overcome her the way it did whenever she was frightened, but she swallowed hard and dredged up a smile as they entered.

Instant silence prevailed.

Mary stood rooted on the threshold, unable to move as seemingly dozens of pairs of eyes locked on her.

Seth took her left arm while Amelia continued to hold her right hand. "This is Mary

McHale," he said to the group. He smiled at her. "You've met some of us, and the rest will introduce themselves when they get a chance to talk to you. Don't worry about remembering names. You'll eventually figure everyone out."

The group called out collective greetings to her and to Jonah, who stepped up close behind her and placed a warm hand in the small of her back. Mary had never been surrounded by protectors before. It felt odd.

The silver-haired gentleman from the restaurant mishap appeared. Beside him was the older woman.

"This is…" Seth began, then paused.

"Uncle Nick," the patriarch said. "And Aunt Fay."

"How do you do?" Mary said.

"Well," Mr. Dalton said in a charming drawl, "I'm doing better than Friday. You sure gave me a turn, gal."

The other Daltons laughed. Zack told his uncle that the older man had given the rest of them a *turn,* too. Mrs. Dalton insisted her husband be seated in a leather easy chair. She took the chair beside him.

"Let's sit and relax," Amelia suggested, releasing Mary and leading the way to the sofa. She sat on one end, Jonah on the other, with Mary settled between them.

"I didn't mean to hurt you," Mary said to the older gentleman. "I was startled when… when we bumped into each other."

Mr. Dalton waved the apology aside. "It was my fault. Looking into your eyes was like looking into the past."

She nodded, not sure what to say.

"Seth and Zack told me your story," he continued. "It's sad what we do to children."

Her throat constricted again. She wondered if she would get through this day with her control intact. The old man's sorrow was in his eyes, and his compassion was a palpable thing, reaching out to her in ways she'd never encountered.

She glanced around the room at all the orphans he'd taken in. The five men were tall, with eyes as blue as periwinkles, except for Seth, the dark one. The lone girl also had the famed Dalton dark hair and blue eyes, but she was petite. And pregnant. So were a couple of the Dalton wives. Among them were two redheads and a couple of blondes, all of whom stood next to their husbands, leaving one man on his own.

A brunette with beautiful brown eyes came to the archway between the living room and kitchen. "Dinner," she said. The lone man smiled at Mary, then went to join the brunette. His wife, Mary assumed, pairing up the couples.

"Good," their aunt said crisply.

Mary soon found herself at a long table set for eight. Mr. Dalton and his wife, Seth, Zack and their wives, and Jonah sat there with her. Mr. Dalton was at the head of the table. Seth seated her on his uncle's right. Jonah was directed to the chair beside her. A round table, glimpsed as she passed the kitchen, accommodated the others.

After the patriarch said the blessing, the men discussed ranching and the coming winter weather in relation to ranching. They needed snow for the moisture content, but hoped it didn't fall in thick blizzards.

"How's business at your place?" Mr. Dalton asked Jonah.

"Pretty good. We're booked solid for the hunting season."

"It's the same with the lodge in town," Seth said. "Zack and I have been sort of managing the place, with Amelia and Honey pitching in, but with our other work increasing, we need to find a full-time manager, especially if we stay open all year in the future."

"We're closing the week before Christmas and don't plan to reopen until spring hiking season," Zack explained.

"Where are all the people coming from?" Mrs. Dalton wanted to know. "Did you notice the new construction around the lake and in town?"

Mary listened to the news of the small community and its increasing growth, both as a vacation center and a mecca for the new businesses coming in to support that growth. This meant additional homes and schools for families and their children. And infrastructure, Seth added.

While Mary had formed lasting ties with two friends from the orphanage and they'd kept in touch by e-mails, she'd never been part of a community the way these people were, their roots spreading deep in the rocky soil for generations.

Her introspection was broken by a couple bringing in bowls of hot food. "Hi, I'm Trevor," one of the Dalton men told her. He carried platters of sliced ham and turkey breast. "This is my wife, Lyric."

"Lyric is my grandniece," Mrs. Dalton explained.

"Aunt Fay raised my father when my grandparents died," Lyric told Mary, serving her and Jonah, then the elder Daltons before passing the bowl of mashed potatoes to the rest. "We're from Texas. That's where Trevor and I met."

Mary recalled the information the waitress had given them at the restaurant yesterday. "You were recently married," she said. "That's what you were celebrating when your uncle and I ran into each other."

Trevor started his two platters around the table after serving the guests and the elders. "Hey, that's right." He beamed a smile at her as if she were a schoolgirl who'd given the correct answer in class.

It was so infectious, Mary found herself

smiling, too. "The waitress said you were the last of the Dalton bachelors."

"She was pretty irked that you went for an out-of-towner," Jonah told the newly married man, a smile playing at the corners of his mouth.

Trevor glanced at his wife. "Well," he said softly, "that's the way it happens sometimes."

Lyric smiled a little and blushed a lot as she served their uncle from the bowl of green beans. Another couple brought in the next dishes and introduced themselves as Travis and Alison.

Mary glanced quickly from Travis to Trevor. To her, they looked exactly alike.

The group burst into laughter. "Yep," their uncle said, "they're twins. So were my younger brothers. Zack, Trevor and Travis belonged to one twin. Seth, Beau and Veronica belonged to the other."

"Veronica prefers to be called Roni," Zack informed her.

"I see." Mary quickly sorted the names in her mind. Zack was the assistant county sheriff; the twins were his younger brothers. Seth was the attorney, Beau was the doctor and Roni was their sister.

Honey was the wife who went with Zack, Amelia with Seth, Alison and Lyric with the twins. There was one more wife, who belonged to Beau, the doctor. Also Roni's husband. She didn't know their names yet.

Jonah touched her arm lightly. "Don't worry. You'll get them straight sooner or later."

She started to tell him she'd be long gone from the area before that was likely to happen. While the ranches joined, she didn't think she and the Dalton family would be communicating. There would be no reason to. She kept her remarks to herself. By the time the cherry pie and ice cream were served, fatigue had settled around her like a damp cloud descending from the mountains.

"Would you like to see the ranch?" Mr. Dalton asked.

Her heart bunched and jerked. She nodded.

With an unstudied gentlemanly grace, he helped her from the chair and ushered her outside. A cone of silence followed them until they were on the porch, then talk resumed inside.

"The original homestead burned in a grass fire around the turn of the last century," the patriarch told her, leading the way across a small front lawn to the horse rail.

They stopped and observed the house.

"The log cabin was rebuilt and added to over the years. It had four rooms, but the kids removed the walls and opened it into a living room that could hold all of us. I added the east wing when I married…the first time," he added. "Later the boys built on the west wing. And Roni. She was always in the thick of things."

"It must have been fun, being part of a big family and working together," she said sincerely.

"Was it bad in the orphanage?"

She shook her head. "Not after I got used to it. We were sort of a great big family, too."

"How many children were there?"

"Well, around fifty of us were permanent. Another twenty-five to thirty came and went as their family fortunes waxed and waned."

Mr. Dalton gave her a questioning glance.

"Prison," she explained. "Drug rehab. Problem parents, we called them." She smiled at the little joke shared privately among the children. "We had little ones, too. The babies were adopted out, if possible. Couples always wanted babies."

He looked so sad Mary was sorry she'd mentioned it. However, he turned them toward the stables. They ambled over to the paddock fence. Several horses came over to sniff them and be petted.

"Zack and the twins do a good job of training the ponies. We raise the best cutting horses in the state. Zack brought in a new stud from Texas, a thoroughbred with great lineage. Next year we'll have his offspring and find out if the mix in bloodlines works."

She knew all about bloodlines. "The registered thoroughbreds all trace back to the three original Arabian barbs brought to England centuries ago. Their pedigrees are more impressive than most people's genealogy."

He was silent for a moment as if he considered every nuance of her words. "It takes more than ancestors to make a person. It's what we are inside that counts—integrity, kindness, a willingness to work for your dream. I understand you're training a jumper?"

The change of subject rattled her a bit. "Uh, yes. I had this insane idea of making the Olympics."

Which seemed really insane when said aloud to another person, she realized.

"Sometimes a person has to face reality, too," she tacked on to show she wasn't totally hopeless when it came to being practical. "Attila pulled a tendon."

"Attila is your stallion?"

"Yes. Attila the Dun. He's dun-colored," she hastened to explain the pun on the name. "He wasn't very good as a racehorse, so I changed his name, a sort of new start for him without past humiliations tagging along."

"A wise, compassionate decision," he murmured, sounding as if she'd done something profound and life-changing.

A blush burned her ears and cheeks.

"The bane of a fair-skinned person," he said, his smile kind so that she suddenly wanted to cry as he briefly touched her face, then dropped his hand. "If my daughter were here, I hope she would be like you."

She recoiled, stunned. "I'm n-not your daughter. I remember my father."

"Tell me about him," he said, leading the way to the side of the house and along a path to the back.

There, a creek ran along a rocky bed shaded by cottonwoods. A bench nestled under one of the bigger trees. He sat and invited her with a gesture to join him. She did so.

Listening to the cheerful flow of the tiny stream, she let her mind drift backward into memories of long ago. Here in this sheltered quiet, she didn't feel threatened as a scene came into her inner vision.

"I remember riding in a truck. A black pickup. Sometimes he had to work on it to keep it running. He always got it going again, so he must have been a good mechanic. We drifted around the West. He took odd jobs here and there."

"What was his name?"

"Cal," she said without thinking. Her heart beat so hard it hurt her chest. "His name was Cal."

"Do you remember his last name?"

Closing her eyes, she stayed in the mental vision, a thing she'd never done because it had been too scary for a child. "No. I don't think he ever told me."

"Was he your father?"

Every nerve in her body jerked at the question. "I don't know. I mean…everyone thought so. Yes, he must have been. Who else could he be?"

"The abductor of a three-year-old?" he suggested softly.

She stood, her hands clenched. A confusing swirl of emotions poured through her. Anger came to the fore. "That's ridiculous!"

"Why?"

"Because." She pressed shaky fingers to her throbbing temples. "He had to be my father. I can't remember a time when he wasn't there, when I wasn't with him."

Mr. Dalton rose, too. "Three is very young." He nodded toward the path along the creek and started walking. "Did you call him Daddy? Or Cal?"

"Cal." Mary followed along the path. "I called him by his name." Somehow she knew this was true.

A fragment of memory came to her—Cal

hitting her, the blow landing on her shoulder as she ducked away. *He's not my daddy,* she'd yelled. *I won't go with him.*

Somehow she knew she was talking to Cal about another man. The man had given Cal money, but he'd snatched it back, saying he wasn't paying for a brat. Then he'd stalked off.

Mary clamped a hand over her mouth, stifling the cry that nearly escaped her. She breathed deeply, forcing her heart rate to slow and become steady, grabbing at composure before the man in front turned her way and startling blue eyes saw into the terror and anguish trapped in a child's soul as the man she'd assumed was her father had tried to sell her.

The earth heaved under her feet, the way it had when she'd first gazed upon the seven peaks that gave the ranch its name. Something was happening inside her, something she didn't understand, couldn't control. Panic spiraled off into her innermost being.

"I have to go," she said, turning back on the trail and rushing toward the house. "There are chores. I have to go home."

Jonah seemed to know of her distress as soon as she and the elder Dalton returned. He and Zack stood on the porch, talking quietly together. They stopped when Mary appeared.

"Are you ready to go?" he asked her.

She nodded.

Mr. Dalton caught up and leaned against the railing. "I hope you'll come back to visit soon. I think we have more to discuss, don't you?"

"That would be…nice," she managed to say. She couldn't meet his eyes. He was somehow part of the turmoil inside her. She didn't know why.

She didn't stop trembling until she was safe in her own room at the hunting lodge.

Chapter Eight

Mary changed clothes and escaped to the ranch chores soon after she and Jonah arrived at the lodge. He had customers in the store and a shrilly ringing telephone to answer, so she was on her own. She had things to think about.

Cal. With the name came other memories of her life with him. Cal had hit her several more times after the man had taken his money and left them. Would a father, a true father, try to sell his only child?

She wanted to believe he couldn't possibly have been her dad, but that could be the desperate illusion of a lonely heart. Children needed to believe they were loved and wanted, but she'd learned in the orphanage that people deserted their families all the time.

She studied the plant so she could identify it next time she saw it.

"It's a common name is two-grooved milkvetch," Jonah told her. "It belongs to the pea family. Not all of the vetches are poisonous, but many are. There's another plant ranchers call crazyweed, also of the pea family, that's poisonous. We have to watch out for it, too."

She mounted up when he did. "What do you use to kill it?"

"Vinegar." He turned the horse toward the stable.

"Vinegar?"

"It's an effective herbicide and much stronger than the grocery variety. The feed and seed store in town carries it." He clicked his pony into a run.

"Is there anything we can do for the cattle?" Mary asked when they reined in at the stable.

"We'll try giving 'em a dose of electrolytes. Otherwise we'll just have to wait and see if they can throw off the glucosides on their own. If they've eaten very much of the weed, then nothing will work."

"Uh, shouldn't we call the vet?"

His glance ridiculed the idea. "Ranchers can't afford to call out a vet every time a cow sneezes."

She realized she needed to read up on bovine illnesses, weeds and other ranching hazards. At the tracks, vets had always been on hand to minister to the high-priced racehorses at the slightest sign of a problem, but apparently that wasn't the case here.

"Right," she said briskly.

From the storage room he gathered the electrolytic kits she was familiar with, plus some wire, rods and a battery. He stored the items in the pickup, added several more, then gestured for her to get in.

Back in the field, she efficiently ran the tube down the yearling's throat and administered the liquid that might help stabilize its metabolism enough for it to recover. Jonah did the same to the cow, then helped with the heifer that threshed about and hindered Mary's efforts.

Finished, they moved the cattle away from the area and set up an electric fence to keep them out.

"We'll spray down the area in the morning. The sun, with the vinegar, will make quick work of the weeds."

"Will it kill the grass, too?"

"Yes. We'll reseed in a couple of weeks. Let's see if we can move these three."

The cow, heifer and yearling were moved in with the rest of the herd after some prodding and heavy lifting on their part. Both she and Jonah had sweat running down their faces by the time they finished. He hooked up the battery to the fence.

"Watch," he said quietly, coming to stand beside her.

A heifer stared at the wire mounted to rods with insulating attachments. She ambled over to it. Finally unable to stand it any longer, she stuck her nose to the wire to see what it was.

Mary saw the spark arc to the damp nose. Three things happened in rapid order. The young cow's tail went straight up; she let out a snort that blew a wad of mucus from her nostrils a good ten feet; a bellow of surprised outrage rent the air. The heifer ran fifty feet from the fence, then turned to stare balefully at it again.

"Okay," Jonah said, "it's working." He glanced at her face and burst out laughing. "You've never seen how cattle react to the electric fence when it's still a novelty?"

As she shook her head another nosy critter went over to check out the fence. A similar reaction occurred.

Still chuckling, Jonah swung into the pickup, waited for her to get in and buckle up, then headed for the lodge.

Glancing over her shoulder at the cattle's antics—by now, ten of them were approaching the wire—she allowed a smile at their silliness. At the house, she followed her boss inside. She realized how tiring the day had been when she went up to her room for the night.

JONAH HEARD THE creak of a squeaky step, then that of a floorboard in the hall sometime after eleven. The wrangler, it appeared, wasn't sleeping.

Meeting the Daltons and talking to their uncle had been a difficult experience for a person who wasn't easy around a lot of people to begin with. Neither she nor Uncle Nick had commented upon their discussion when they'd returned to the house, and no one had been foolish enough to ask.

Mary had requested to leave at once. The old man had been unusually silent. His family, taking their cue from him, had bide Mary goodbye in a subdued manner.

Jonah had sensed turmoil in Mary on the trip back to their place. He wondered what her perceptions of the Dalton gang were. Ah, well. It was none of his business.

It was also none of his business that she couldn't sleep. He willed himself to stay where he was and try to get some shut-eye himself. When the light from the kitchen spilled across the lawn and reflected into his room, he sighed, rose and pulled on a pair of sweats and a T-shirt.

Mary started upon seeing him arrive at the kitchen doorway. She recovered quickly. "Would you like some hot chocolate?" she asked in her polite manner.

"Sure."

He studied her as she prepared another cup. When it was ready, she handed it to him, then went into the dining room. He flicked off the light and followed. The dim light of the hall sconces, which stayed on all night, barely brightened the room. When his vision adjusted to the dark, he could see the pale wash of moonlight across the lawn and outbuildings.

"It's getting colder at night," he said. "Autumn, then winter, will be here before we know it."

"If winter comes, can spring be far behind?" she quoted from some literary saying he vaguely remembered from college.

"Do you want to talk about it?"

"About what?"

He was disappointed at her evasive tactic. "Whatever is keeping you awake. I assume it's because of your talk with Uncle Nick."

"Not really," she said coolly.

"Then you must have remembered something else from your childhood." He sipped the cocoa, found it didn't burn his tongue and took a swallow.

Her eyes cut to him, then returned to the outdoor scene. She didn't answer.

Something told him he should leave well enough alone. Her life, memories, whatever, weren't his concern. As usual, he didn't listen to the inner voice of common sense. "What was it?" he asked, persisting in the inquisition.

She sampled her cocoa and took her sweet time before replying. "My father's name was Cal. He tried to…sell me to another man once. He told me to call the man Daddy. I think it was a black market adoption."

Although her voice was steady and precise, Jonah recognized the emotional tension when she had to pause in the middle of her explanation. He admired the way she refused to let herself stutter over the word.

Her smile cut into him when she glanced his way. "Maybe I should have gone with the man. He must have been rich. He gave Cal a lot of money for me."

"Honey—"

"On the other hand," she went on as if telling a story, "I wouldn't have known the fun and freedom of living with Mary if I'd gone with him."

Her stubborn aloofness was part of the defense she'd built long ago. It made him angry that a child had had to erect all those barriers in order to survive. And yes, he felt pity for her. Her life had been difficult and dangerous.

"Yeah, there was that," he said.

They finished the cocoa in silence. She took the cups to the kitchen, placed them in the sink and filled them with water. "Good night," she said, passing him in the hallway.

Without thinking, he clasped her forearm. He heard the quick gasp she gave as she froze. "It doesn't have to hurt forever," he told her softly, wanting to be gentle with her at the same time he wanted to crush her to him. "You can find enough happiness to make it go away."

He didn't understand his own motives as he stroked through the unbound silky length of her hair. He brought a strand to his lips. It was soft and warm. She smelled of shampoo and good things. Womanly things.

"If I kissed you," he murmured, "would you hit me or run away?"

"Both, in that order."

Her manner was amused but defiant, a challenge that he wanted to answer. Neither of them moved.

He took a deep breath and tried to let her

go, to get past the moment of madness. It was no use. Slowly, so she could run if she needed to, he bent to her.

He kissed her cheek, then her temple. He slipped both hands into her hair and cupped her head in his palms. He lowered his head, seeking her lips, needing the warmth, the taste of her...

"No," she said.

She pushed him away with both hands on his chest. He let her go, breathing harshly as if he'd grazed on locoweed and could no longer get air into his lungs. She rushed up the stairs and into her room. The lock snicked into place behind her.

He tried to figure out what had possessed him to indulge the urgings of desire like that. Stupid. Really stupid. He'd learned the rules of self-preservation long ago. Giving in to passion wasn't on the list.

MARY GLANCED UP when Jonah entered the kitchen the next morning.

The panicky sensations of the previous day rushed through her, along with the new, strange need to lean into him and know his strength was there for her. She forced the emotions into the lockbox with the old, painful memories and slammed the lid shut tight. Without meeting his sharp gaze, she continued kneading the dough on the floured wax paper until it was no longer sticky.

"What's that?" he asked.

"Sourdough. I haven't made it in years. It's a base for biscuits, bread, dinner rolls. I thought the hunters would like it."

"Right. Uh, look, I'm sorry for last night. I don't know what happened. I don't usually step over the line."

She shrugged. "It was because of what happened with the cattle and working together to try to save them. It breeds a sort of intimacy that's hard to resist."

He poured a cup of coffee. "Got it all figured out, huh?"

Giving him an oblique glance to assess his mood, she covered the dough and set it aside to rise, then threw the wax paper in the trash and wiped up the dusting of flour on the counter. "I read a lot of psychology books at one time. I wanted to understand what made people tick."

"Like how a father could sell his own kid?"

His blunt question hurt in more ways than she could count. She waited a few seconds before replying, until she could be sure she wouldn't display any emotion. "I didn't remember that episode until yesterday."

Jonah leaned against the sink edge and sipped the steaming coffee. She didn't like the way his eyes could see past the facade that normally kept others at arm's length. She didn't like the way he probed, considered her reply, then probed some more.

"But the memory was there," he said. "Many memories. Kidnapped, an attempted black market sale, abandonment, living mostly on your own with the old woman, then in the orphanage."

He turned abruptly and stared out the window, but not before she saw the fierce frown he wore. This was getting too serious again. "Well, as they say, what doesn't kill you makes you stronger."

He was beside her in three strides. The cup rapped loudly on the counter when he set it down. She half flinched when he clasped her upper arms.

"Dammit, I won't hurt you," he said in a snarl.

There was a promise in the words. She suddenly worried that he would. He was smart and tough, but he was also compassionate. He would have cared about that little girl who tried not to show the world how frightened she was.

"I know." She looked him in the eye so he would know she didn't need anyone's sympathy. "No one can."

"Because you don't let them get close enough?"

She heaved a breath as he returned to probing for more than she wanted to disclose. "Exactly. Also, I wasn't kidnapped."

"You were if you're the Dalton girl."

"I'm not."

"How do you know?"

"Because if Cal wanted money for me, why wouldn't he have collected a ransom? I think Mr. Dalton would have paid whatever it took to get his daughter back."

"Maybe he already had the other deal set up," Jonah suggested, dropping his hands and stepping back an inch. "Then you carried on so, the other man backed out."

She gave him a sardonic grin. "There are advantages to being a brat."

"Maybe."

She was aware of the way his eyes flicked over her face, taking in all parts and putting them together in his mind in a conclusion she couldn't read. Breathing was hard when he stared at her as if her soul was his for the taking.

"There are DNA tests," he murmured.

"For what?"

"To see if you really are a Dalton."

"No! I mean, there's no need. I remember everything that happened to me from the time I was three. If I'd been here before, I would have recognized it. I would have known the place I called home…"

She let the words trail away. Yesterday on the trip to the Dalton ranch, she'd had an odd feeling where the road wound up the thickly forested slope. The big meadow below it had beckoned to her. She could almost see herself, and other children, too, running through the grass and wildflowers.

Perhaps it was a scene from her orphanage days when spring was blooming over the land and the children had run through the sunshine, happy that winter was over.

"Would you?" he questioned. "A three-year-old who'd been in an auto accident, her mother killed? If a stranger stopped to see what had happened and then took her away, wouldn't she think he was taking her home?"

She shot him a dark glare to let him know she didn't want to discuss it further.

"You may have been hurt. You certainly would have been frightened. With all else gone, you would have clung to the one constant in your rapidly changing world—your abductor."

"You seem to have the psychology of the moment worked out," she said in a scoffing voice.

"In marketing we had to know our audience."

She slipped past him and refreshed the cool coffee in her cup. "When do I get paid?"

He scowled when she changed the subject, but he dropped the intense search into her psyche. "On the first of each month. Do you need some money now?"

"No. I just wanted to be clear on it."

He gave a skeptical snort. "And to remind me of the line between boss and wrangler. Sorry. You've stirred up a lot of questions in my mind. I don't like not knowing the answers."

"Neither do I," she admitted, "but it isn't your problem. Or your business."

"True."

She inhaled slowly, finding it was hard to make a request. "After we spray out the vetch and I finish the chores, may I have some time off?"

His prolonged study caused her to think he was going to refuse, but he nodded. "Take the rest of the day. You've worked hard enough without a break since you arrived."

"Thanks."

After an early lunch, Mary left in the SUV. She passed Jonah in the campground and felt only slightly guilty that she wasn't helping him police the area and replenish the wood supply for the campfire pits. All the weekend campers had left, except for one tent site.

He waved as she drove by, then stood there, his eyes narrowed against the noon sun as she followed the road he'd taken the previous day. At the saddle where they'd stopped, she paused and surveyed the land.

Behind her were the red and beige cliffs of the Towbridge place. For some reason, the boundary represented safety to her. If she went forward, she would be on Dalton land.

She let off the brake and eased the SUV down the road. The big meadow came into view, also the wooded slope bisected by the gravel road. She stopped halfway up the hill.

A tiny creek crossed the road through a culvert and disappeared into the trees.

The quiet, after she turned off the engine, was enormous. It weighed on her as she made her way down a faint trail through the woods. A jaybird squawked directly overhead, causing every muscle in her body to jump.

Stopping, she listened to the rush of her own breath and the increased tempo of her heartbeat. She knew, without knowing how she knew, what lay beyond the edge of the forest.

As silently as possible, she continued down

the trail that followed the creek, then gasped when she stepped into the clearing at the edge of the meadow.

The cabin stood as silent and still as a sentinel, weathered and wise, waiting...waiting for her.

Yesterday, passing along the road, she'd felt she'd been here before. Last night, visions of a cabin had haunted her until she'd known she had to see for herself.

And here it was.

Feeling like a lonely Gretel, she forced her feet to move until she stood before the wooden door. A stick wedged into the latch was easy to remove. She went inside.

The cabin, shaded by the trees from the morning sun, was cool. Dust motes spun in a beam of light from a window, stirred by the opening of the door.

Like the line shack on the Towbridge ranch, this cabin had a couple of bunk beds, a table, two chairs and a potbellied stove. A wooden box contained firewood and some old papers and magazines. Shelves were lined with canned goods and staples. Matches and a lantern filled with kerosene were available.

A lone lightbulb with a dingy shade was attached to the wall.

Hearing laughter, she spun around. No one was there.

Not now, but once there had been. She knew that children had once run through this meadow, laughing and carefree, that she'd been with them.

Someone…a tall, strong man…had lifted her in front of him onto a saddle. They'd ridden across the meadow as fast as the wind. She'd laughed and shouted, "Giddyup, horsey!"

She went outside and gazed at the tall bunch grass waving in the breeze. "I know this place," she whispered. "I know this place, those children…that man."

Her heart felt as if it would burst. She sat on the flat rock that formed the stoop, dropped her hat to the ground and laid her head on her knees. The warmth of the sun caressed her scalp and shoulders, soothed the unnamed fears.

She needed comforting, she realized, hearing once more the distant laughter of the children, not sure if it had been real or not, no longer sure she'd been part of it.

But she wanted to be, so much so that she ached with a need for something she couldn't name.

After a long time, the memory—delusion?—faded and her heart eased somewhat. Growing sleepy after the restless night, she went inside and lay on the hard mattress of a bunk. The quiet surrounded her, enfolded her, lifted her in a sweet embrace and rocked her to sleep.

It was dark when she awoke. The breeze coming in the door was no longer warm or soothing. It was downright cold.

Mary rose stiffly and remembered where she was. However none of the certainty of déjà vu that had driven her to this remote place remained. The children's laughter was gone.

A dark mist was descending along the slopes of the mountains. From far away, she saw the crackle of lightning. It was several seconds before the rumble of thunder reached her.

Quickly she closed up the cabin, grabbed

her hat and jammed it over her tangled hair, then dashed up the trail to her vehicle. She wanted to get home before the storm descended in case the road washed out or was flooded.

At the crest of the saddle, she looked for the red cliff but it wasn't visible. The mist had already moved into the valley. Flicking on the headlights and windshield wipers, she peered through the deepening gloom, a sense of urgency pushing at her every mile of the way.

Behind her, the clouds swirled and thickened. Mocking her childish fears, she dispelled the notion that the Headless Horseman would come galloping out of the dust at any moment.

"Silly," she said, needing the sound of a human voice, even if it was only hers, to break the mood.

When the lights of the lodge twinkled at her through the trees of the camping area, she was relieved.

Home.

Well, not exactly, but for the duration of her employment, it was close enough.

The rain poured down when she pulled up

before the old bunkhouse and turned off the engine. She sat in the truck and listened to its fury for several minutes. When it showed no signs of letting up, she decided to return to the horse rail in front of the lodge and park there for the night.

She did so, then reached for a jacket on the crew seat behind her. With it over her head, she leaped from the SUV and onto the broad front porch, glad that it had a roof.

The front door opened and a tall figure was framed in its rectangle of light. "Where the hell have you been?" an extremely irritated masculine baritone asked.

Chapter Nine

Mary peered into eyes as stormy as the weather. Then she did something that surprised them both. She slid her arms around Jonah and nestled her face against his throat, instinctively seeking the heat of his body to warm her as she'd earlier sought the warmth of the sun.

"Mary?" he said in a low, husky tone.

She didn't answer.

His chest lifted against hers in a deep breath, then his arms encircled her, pulling her closer until she could feel their hearts beating together.

"Come in," he murmured, nuzzling his nose into her hair. "Come in from the storm."

She let him pull her inside and lock the door behind them. The storm was shut out, and she felt safe.

"You're cold. What happened? Did you get stuck?" he asked, taking her arm and leading her to the sofa. A blaze licked hotly over the huge logs in the fireplace.

"No. I'm fine. Just cold."

He wrapped an afghan around her shoulders and pushed her onto the sofa. After removing her boots, he sat beside her and rubbed her feet until they were warm again.

"Sit still. I'll bring some hot tea."

Nodding, she curled into the corner of the deep sofa and, laying her head on the plush fabric, closed her eyes.

Minutes or eons later, she heard Jonah return. "Here," he said. "This'll take the chill out."

When she sipped the hot liquid, a different kind of warmth slid down her throat. She coughed as the brandy fumes filled her lungs. "You should warn a person of surprises," she managed to say when she could breathe once more.

He sampled the brew. "I think I got carried away with my good intentions." He brought a ceramic teapot in and topped off their cups, then added more honey to hers.

"Better?" he asked.

She tasted and nodded. "Much."

His gaze roamed over her. "You were gone a long time. I was getting worried."

"I'm sorry. I went to sleep."

"In your truck?"

She shook her head. "There's a cabin on the Dalton property, past the saddle and down the next hill."

"An emergency cabin. All ranches have them."

"When we passed that area on the way to their house, I felt something. I wasn't sure what it was, but I had to return. I wanted to see if I could remember anything, in case I'd been there before, when I was a child."

He settled on the sofa beside her and propped his sock-clad feet on the low table. "Did you?"

She sighed. "I don't know." She stared into the fire as if searching in a crystal ball. "It's odd, but since coming here, I seem to recall children and...and laughter. It makes me sad. I don't know why. Isn't that strange?"

"Maybe. Did you expect the cabin to be there?"

"Yes." She sipped the spiked tea while she

considered the turmoil of the afternoon and tried to shake off the lingering trace of sadness. "I knew what it would look like. I was positive I'd seen it before, but later I wasn't so sure."

Jonah finished the warm drink and set his cup on the coffee table. When she was done, he offered her more tea. She shook her head and handed him her cup to place beside his.

After adding two more logs to the fire, he rejoined her, pulling her feet close so they rested on his thigh. He wore a sweat outfit in navy-blue, and she could feel the flex of hard muscles through the material and her socks.

She let her head slide forward until it rested on his shoulder. Turning toward her, he gathered her close with an arm around her shoulders and lifted her legs so they lay across his lap. He rested his head against the sofa and closed his eyes with a contented sigh.

Slowly her eyelids became too heavy to hold up. They drifted down, but she wasn't asleep. For now it was nice just to sit there before the fire and listen to the storm outside, her soul at peace after the disturbing afternoon.

"HONEY, IT'S ALMOST midnight. Time to go to bed."

Mary woke, not sure where she was. Jonah lay in the corner of the sofa. She rested against him, nearly on top of him, in fact. The position was too intimate, too trusting.

"I'm sorry," she said, unable to believe she'd fallen asleep tucked into his arms.

"I'm not." He rubbed her neck and into her scalp, stopping her when she would have moved.

Not that she wanted to. She knew she should. But she couldn't. "I'm not like this," she told him, trying to sound firm and sure and strong.

"I know." He kissed the top of her head, his lips barely skimming over her hair, then onto her forehead, leaving a trail of pleasant heat.

She liked it. A lot. Lifting her face, she invited more. It had been a long time since she'd invited anyone's touch. Being close suddenly didn't seem such a weak and vulnerable thing. Not with this man.

The kiss went on and on. When he gathered her into his arms and wrapped one leg over hers, she let him. He rolled to a new position, holding her so that she nestled against the sofa back and his body partially covered hers, a full embrace that filled a need she hadn't wanted to acknowledge.

His hands, large and capable, moved over her. She shifted against him, wanting more.

"We can go as far as you want," he said. "Just be sure you want it."

Her mind was already made up, although she didn't know when that had happened. Perhaps when she slept. "I do."

He lifted away from her enough to make some adjustments to his clothing. She felt a coolness wash across her torso when he unfastened her shirt buttons, then his hand pushed her T-shirt upward so that he could touch her skin.

She felt as if she might burst, but not from the earlier painful emotions. This time it was passion that filled her, like a wind sweeping through a field of wildflowers. Like a flower, she responded to the sunny warmth of his touch.

After tossing his sweatshirt aside, he settled against her, a strip of bare skin on each of them coming together as he adjusted his length to hers. The hard urgency of his body caused a new storm of desire to swell within.

"This doesn't mean anything," she said.

She felt his laughter. "I think that's my line." He nibbled on her earlobe.

When his hand closed over her breast, she squeezed her eyes tightly closed and let her other senses take over.

Outside, the storm lashed at the sturdy lodge as if the seven devil monsters of old had been freed and demanded their due. They raised their banshee wails into shrieks that careened around the eaves, demanding entrance.

"The wind is hungry," she said.

He lifted his head and gazed into her eyes. "So am I. I didn't know how much."

She nodded solemnly. It was the same for her. She sighed shakily and pressed her nose into the groove of his neck, inhaling deeply, needing the scent of him in her. Sliding her hands under his shirt, she explored the smooth flesh of his back, finding the flex and strength of his muscular torso very enticing.

When he shifted his leg to slide one thigh between hers, she realized their clothing was in the way. She tugged at her shirt and made a little sound of impatience.

"Good idea," he said, his tone husky, sexy.

He sat up, then cupped her face in his hands and kissed her mouth several times, quick, teasing forays that left her hungry for more. She bit at his lips until he gave her a real kiss, with just enough tongue to satisfy her for the moment.

Smiling when she protested, he released her mouth and sat up. "Let's go to bed, Mary. It's getting cold out here."

As soon as she nodded, he stood and, taking her hand, helped her to her feet. Looping an arm around her waist and flicking off the lamp as they passed the table, he led her to the sunroom. There he closed the curtains, which dimmed the howl of the wind and softened the onslaught of the rain and occasional tap of hail against the panes.

In the darkness, she felt his hands return and make quick work of her clothing, then his own. He again held her close. This time skin met only skin.

"You feel good," he murmured. "Like warm silk."

She dared to tease him. "So do you." She ran her fingers over his chest.

His quick intake of breath when she traced her fingers down his body, past his waistline, pleased her. A gentle nudge against her abdomen assured her of his desire. Her own hunger surged, making her stronger, bolder. She rested her hands at his hips and leaned into him the tiniest bit, just until her breasts made contact. Then she hesitated and gazed at him in the dim light.

"Keep doing whatever pleases you," he murmured. "I can be patient."

His voice was husky. It glided over her like buttered syrup, soothing the faint riffs of alarm that questioned the wisdom of being with him like this. The quick flash of his smile reassured her. They could stop at any time. They could go so far, then back off. It was up to her.

Grateful, she leaned a little more, then moved slowly up and down, back and forth. Her nipples became achy points of sensation. Electricity spiraled down, down, down to the innermost parts of her, past fear and caution and self-preservation.

His hands moved from her shoulder to her back, along her spine to her hips. A shudder went through him when she pressed closer with the lower part of her body, bringing them into greater contact there while she continued the light strokes of her breast against him. Passion flared and glowed, opening like the heart of a volcano inside her. She wanted him…she wanted…him. Just him.

When the hunger became too great, they moved as one, wrapping each other in the snug embrace of their arms, their lips seeking, finding, merging. She was intensely aware of him, of his body and her own. They touched at all the erotic points—mouths, chests, bellies, thighs. He opened his stance in order to enclose her legs between his, guided his hardness between her thighs.

She moved against him and felt the slick heat of her own passion, moist and inviting, telling him that her need was as great as his. Tremors echoed through her. When they threatened to buckle her knees, she whispered, "I think I'm going to fall."

He chuckled. Lifting the sheet, a thermal blanket and a heavier wool coverlet with Native American designs, he tucked her in the large bed and slid in beside her. Meshing their legs, he again lay partially over her and took her mouth in a kiss that went deep, very deep.

She stopping breathing, no longer needing air, wanting only him. She moved her hands over him in restless treks. The hunger grew as they touched more intimately. She was ready for him, she realized.

"Come to me," she demanded.

A shudder went through him. "Give me a sec."

She hated when he moved away, but watched as he removed a condom from the bedside table and secured it. His eyes cut to her, catching her interested observation. She smiled and looked away like a child caught staring.

He touched her reddened cheek with the back of one finger. "This isn't your usual style."

She felt the heat increase. Since they'd both made it clear they didn't get involved, the present circumstances were hard to explain. "Nor yours."

"Yeah. You're the exception to my golden rule."

She knew what he meant. It was another mystery to add in with the others she'd discovered since coming here.

He stretched out on his side, sliding their legs together again, and laid a hand on her hip, his thumb rubbing slowly over her. He studied her face, not in an intrusive way, but as if he found her fascinating.

"Am I making you self-conscious?" he asked. "It's hard not to stare."

"Why?" While she didn't consider herself a flaming beauty, she knew men seemed intrigued by her eyes.

He traced her eyebrow with his finger. "Your eyes are beautiful, startling so. But it's more than that." He tipped her chin up and studied her in the dim light from the sconces left on the hallway. "You're wary. Everything about you says 'don't come close.' It makes a man want to do just that."

She managed a laugh. "So it's the challenge?"

He leaned close and kissed her lightly.

"That's part of the attraction, but I outgrew the need to kiss and conquer long ago."

His statement surprised and confused her, but his lips didn't. He moved over her face, her neck, her throat, laving sweet, damp kisses and licks along her skin. It worried her that she wanted him like this, that the need, when she'd returned to the lodge, had been so strong.

"Don't think so much," he told her, his smile full of understanding and amusement.

He shifted again, bringing her on top of him. When she rested on her elbows, her face directly over his, he arranged her hair around them.

"Just like I imagined," he murmured.

She realized then that she wanted the world to go away. She wanted to cling to him until nothing could separate them. That seemed odder than her feelings of the afternoon.

Would there be regret in the morning?

Pressing her face against him, she kissed his throat, his chest, along his collarbone, while he caressed her sides and hips, through her hair. They would deal with tomorrow when it came, she decided just before the red mist of intense passion blanked out all other thought.

When she couldn't stand it another moment, he came to her, his touch sure and gentle, moving slowly, letting her adjust to his masculine form without force or impatience.

He moved when she wanted him to, remained still when she hesitated. He could read her every emotion—the fear of needing another and the need that drove the fear away.

After a long, breathless period, he let them rest, their bodies fully meshed and perfectly joined. As if they'd been made for each other.

He must have thought so, too. "Perfect," he murmured at one point. "We're perfect together."

"Yes. I...I want you. Now."

Looking into her eyes, he began to move, slowly, then faster as the heat built. She couldn't look away.

"Oh," she murmured and bit into her lower lip, holding back, not quite ready for it to end.

"There'll be more," he promised in a hoarse whisper. "Take everything. We'll have it all."

She wasn't sure what he was vowing or what she was promising in return as she held onto him as hard as she could, needing him as an anchor for the storm that raged within the innermost part of her. Through it all, fear licked at the back of the passion, receding but never going away. She knew…she knew she shouldn't need, she shouldn't want, she shouldn't hope…

Then it didn't matter as he carried her along the swift, dark road to passion, to the culmination of desire. She cried out, then whispered wearily, "Jonah, hold me."

"I will, honey. I've got you. Trust me."

She nodded, boneless now that the hunger was sated. Snuggling close, she closed her eyes and sleep, wonderful restful sleep, crept over her.

"MARY, WAKE UP. You're dreaming."

Mary's eyes snapped open. They were damp as if she'd been crying. Jonah was peering at her in the gray light of dawn.

The room was cold. She shivered.

"A nightmare?" he asked, coaxing her to share.

"It was so real," she said. "There was someone. A child. She was called Tinkerbell."

He nodded, his gaze never leaving hers.

"Tinkerbell," she repeated in a choked whisper. "That was me. I think. But when? I wasn't called Tinkerbell at the orphanage." She shook her head. "No, not Tinkerbell... Tink...once I was called Tink. The children in the meadow—"

With the words, the past became clearer. Once she'd been three and she'd been called Tink by those children, by that strong, laughing man. Tears flooded her eyes.

She blinked them away and stared at Jonah in confusion. Something strange was happening to her. She could no longer distinguish between what was real and what wasn't.

"Tink?" His hand tightened on her shoulder as he demanded softly but with an incredulous undertone, "Tink?"

"It was my nickname. A long time ago. When I was with Cal. I could only remember two things—that I was three and that my name was Tink. He said it wasn't a real name and that I wasn't to use it anymore."

Jonah was silent as he studied her. "I think," he finally said, "that we'd better put on a pot of coffee and have a talk."

When he rose, dressed and went to the kitchen, she grabbed her clothes and rushed up the stairs. She showered and dressed, then returned downstairs. It was necessary, in her mind, to erase the remnants of the passionate night before she faced the reality of the day.

Jonah knew something that she didn't. She thought it was going to be bad news.

JONAH LEANED AGAINST the counter and sipped the freshly-brewed coffee while waiting for Mary…Tink…whoever the heck she was. He shook his head and cast a wary glance toward the dining room and the window there that gave a view of the east. The sun was almost over the horizon.

Good. They needed to shed some light on the situation.

He snorted at the attempt at humor and admitted he felt more like a rube who'd sat in on a poker game well over his head than anything else. Hearing Mary's step, he wondered if his first thoughts about her had been true—that she'd come there seeking clues to her past. He asked that question as soon as she appeared.

She shook her head and poured a cup of coffee. Leaning against the counter opposite him, she contemplated the great outdoors as if her thoughts went no further.

The sadness of yesterday was gone, he noted. In its place was her usual cautious approach to life. Her thoughts were hidden behind the tinted shades she wore. He leaned forward and gestured toward the glasses.

"You won't need those," he said, speaking quietly as he would to a wild creature so it wouldn't bolt.

"What do you know that I don't?" she asked, leaving the shades in place and connecting the dots as usual.

He considered several replies, then realized that only the truth would do between them. "After you and Uncle Nick ran into each other, Zack called. He and Seth wanted to come over and talk to you."

She nodded.

"During the phone conversation, he referred to his missing cousin as Tink."

Her delicate complexion went ashen. He saw her lips part as she sucked in an audible breath. Her hand trembled as she took a drink of coffee. She shook her head as if she didn't believe him.

"It's true."

She rubbed her temple with the fingers of one hand. "This is too bizarre to be real."

"There's something else."

She pressed her lips together and waited.

"I think there is a scar on your thigh. Under the unicorn. I thought I, uh, felt something."

She was silent so long he didn't think she was going to answer. "It's old," she said, "so old, I'd forgotten about it. Other than some barely raised spots, it's hardly there."

"But you remembered it when Uncle Nick mentioned it, didn't you?"

"I realized it was a p-possibility."

The hardly noticeable stutter indicated the stress she tried to conceal. Sympathy stirred in him, and he found he wanted to take her in his arms and protect her from all the hurts of the past and those of the future. When had he become so gallant? he asked himself, amused, exasperated and puzzled about his own see-sawing emotions.

"I think we're going to have to talk to the

Daltons again." He spoke as gently as he could.

"No!"

He gave her time to realize there was no other way.

She gave him one of her stubborn glares. "It's one of those odd coincidences that happen. There's nothing to it. There can't be. I'd remember—"

When she stopped abruptly, he said, "I think you *have* remembered the past, enough of it to disturb you. Don't you want to know the truth?"

She inhaled deeply and released the breath slowly. "I've never found the truth to be very palatable."

Her attempt at ironic amusement tugged at something deep and tender inside him. "You've faced several truths in your lifetime and lived through them. You can make it through this, too."

It took a long minute before she acquiesced. "If I am a Dalton, then what?"

He smiled. "Then I imagine there will be a celebration at the return of the prodigal."

She turned and set the cup on the counter,

her shoulders rigid. He placed his cup beside hers, then laid his hands on her upper arms. "I'll go with you."

Her chin lifted a notch. "I'm not afraid."

"I know, but everyone needs backup once in a while." He kept his tone casual, his touch light, but she was strung as tight as a piano wire near the breaking point.

When she turned toward him, her face held no trace of emotion, but for a second he thought he saw fear in her eyes.

"Do you want to call them, or shall I?" he asked.

The stiffness went out of her spine as she acknowledged there was no other choice. "I will."

He nodded. "Let's go today."

Her smile was fleeting. "Right. We may as well get it over with, I suppose."

He had to laugh. "Finding your long-lost family isn't a life sentence." He paused at her sardonic glance. "I suppose, in a way, it is," he conceded.

"One of the most difficult things about being a ward of the state was the uncertainty," she told him. "We never knew if or when we were going to be placed with a family or in which dorm or with which housemother."

"Were some of them bad?"

"Not really, mostly indifferent or impatient. A couple of them were really nice. We all wanted to be in their houses."

"I think you'll find the Daltons in the last category."

She laced her fingers together against her stomach. "All the kids had dreams. We used to make up stories for each other about our families coming to find us and how wonderful it would be. We would have toys and treats and be happy forever."

He ran his hands up and down her arms, sensing the chill inside her. "Happy forever," he murmured. "I think happiness only comes at odd moments, like finding a four-leaf clover."

"I think you're right." She moved aside.

"The Daltons will be up by now."

She froze for an instant. "Then I'll go make that call."

Jonah stayed in the kitchen while she disappeared down the hall. In the office he heard her ask to speak to Mr. Dalton. He wondered what she would call the older man if they decided she belonged to them.

And if she belonged to them, then where did that leave *him?* Good question. He wasn't ready to give her up—

He broke the thought as a tempest whirled inside him. For a second, he felt as uncertain as a teenager in the throes of first love, then he set about preparing breakfast for them. When she returned to the kitchen, he glanced her way.

"I said we'd be over after the morning chores," she told him. "Mr. Dalton didn't ask any questions."

Seeing what he was doing, she pitched in and buttered the toast when it popped up, the activity restoring her composure and control.

Jonah smiled at her, feeling proud for no reason except her bravery. As if she were his personal protégée. As if he were personally involved. As if…

MARY WONDERED IF Jonah took the long way around by the county road to give her more time to face what was coming when they reached the Seven Devils ranch.

Nothing about this trip seemed real, not the three crows sitting on a fence, the serenity of the day or the man who accompanied her, determined to be at her side as if she needed his support.

Did she?

She closed her eyes as something like panic swirled away inside her. She didn't know what she wanted at this moment, except that it wasn't more complications. She still hadn't figured out last night and why she'd gone to Jonah. Or why he'd let her.

For one insane moment, she wished they were still snuggled in bed and tomorrow would never come.

But it always did.

Opening her eyes, she forced herself to consider that this meeting might change her life forever. It wasn't quite imaginable, and she'd always had a reliable imagination.

The road turned sharply, swinging in a tight arc around a huge rock that blocked the route from going straight.

"Stop," she said. "Please. Stop!"

The tires skidded a bit on the gravel, then

bit in. Jonah brought the vehicle to a halt. "What is it?"

"I want to get out."

Before he could protest or question her, she stepped down from the cab and walked toward the rock. Jonah quietly appeared at her side. He took her hand.

"What do you remember?" he asked softly.

She clung to him. "I think something terrible happened here. Someone was crying."

"Your mother...Tink's mother...was killed on this curve. Something happened, perhaps a deer ran in front of the car, but she slammed on the brakes, went into a skid and hit the rock where it juts out into a wedge."

"She died instantly?"

"Yes."

The pain of it reached deeply into her. She could almost see that child, almost hear her sobs, almost feel her bewilderment as she patted the still face of her mother.

"Jonah," she said.

His response was immediate. "I'm here."

It was hard to say. "I was so scared."

He wrapped her in his arms, holding her

loosely so she could escape if she wanted. "I know, Mary."

"Who am I?" she said.

"We'll find out. When we do, we'll go from there."

"If I'm not Tink, then what?"

"Then you're the wrangler at the Towbridge ranch." He smiled at her. "And I'm your boss and get to order you to go home and get to work."

She heard the question behind the last two words. "That works for me."

"No regrets about last night?"

"No. Why should I have?"

"You might become the pampered daughter of Nicholas Dalton and a member of a First Family of Idaho. Your social circle will expand. Men will beat a path to the ranch house door, seeking your hand."

She recognized the devilish gleam in his eyes. "Huh," she said, recovering her poise, which she was sure he'd meant for her to do. "Sounds like fortune hunters to me."

His chuckle echoed in his chest. Somehow her head rested there as naturally as a bird returning to its nest. She straightened up. He released her and stepped back, perceptive in knowing her need for his comforting touch was over and she was ready to move on. They returned to the truck.

"I'm not sure a three-pointed scar is enough to prove anything," she murmured. "Or a nickname."

"We'll see." He flicked her an assessing glance, smiled at her, then cranked the engine.

Ten minutes later they drove under the welcoming arch of the Seven Devils Ranch. The name was carved into the massive log over the entrance along with a date, 1865.

Roots, she thought. They go back so far, so deeply into the mountain soil. Was this where she sprang from, too?

When the truck stopped, Nick Dalton walked out of the house and stood on the porch, his face solemn, his eyes filled with wisdom and kindness. His wife—Aunt Fay— came out and stood next to him. She laid her hand on his arm when he started forward. He stopped and waited for Mary and Jonah to come to them.

"Good morning," Aunt Fay said. "It's good to see you two again."

Her crisp cheer eased the moment of meeting and she invited them in. Once seated in the living room, the older woman served coffee and offered homemade rolls. Mary declined. Her throat had a tendency to close without notice. She hardly sipped the coffee.

After a moment of silence, Mr. Dalton spoke to her. "Please," he said. "Tell me what you remember."

It was as if he already knew exactly what had happened to her of late.

Glancing at Jonah, who nodded encouragement, she began with the day she'd arrived in town.

Chapter Ten

Mary tried to cover every detail of every fleeting memory since she'd been in the area. When she finished, there was only silence within the house.

Mr. Dalton studied her for a long moment. "Tink had a scar on her left leg, high on the thigh where she fell on a broken bottle."

"I used to wonder how I got it," she said, nodding to admit it was there. "When I wore a bathing suit, people always asked about it. I used to make up stories. Once I said a three-fanged snake had bitten me and I nearly died. The orphanage director made me write an essay about lying."

She smiled when the other three laughed.

"There's one other thing I've thought of. What's your blood type?" Mr. Dalton asked.

"O-negative." Her heart thudded as she waited for his response.

"So am I," he said. "So was your mother."

The reference confused her, then she realized what he was saying. "That isn't proof."

"What more do we need?" Aunt Fay asked, giving her a rather stern perusal. "You look like a Dalton, you act like a Dalton—if stubbornness runs in families and I'm convinced it does—and you have the same blood type. Your early life was shrouded in mystery until you went to the orphanage. Your memories start when you were three, which was the time when Theresa Ann disappeared."

"We can do a DNA test to be sure," the family patriarch suggested.

Mary realized that he and his wife had already made up their minds. Now it was up to her. She turned to Jonah.

"It's your call," he said softly.

"What do you think?" she asked, needing his opinion before she could accept the possible truth.

He stroked her cheek with the back of one finger and paused where the dimple appeared when she smiled. "I have no doubts. You're the missing child." He glanced at Mr. Dalton. "She remembered that her nickname was Tink. She knew where the line shack was by the meadow and recognized the rock where her mother died."

Mr. Dalton rose. "Tink," he whispered hoarsely. "I knew it the first time I looked at you."

Mary surged to her feet. She wanted to bolt. Like the frightened child she'd once been, she wanted to run and never look back. As a three-year-old, her life had taken a strange twist, several of them, now it seemed about to do the same thing all over again. When the older man reached for her, she stiffened, unable to stop the reaction.

He dropped his arms, pain in his face.

"I'm sorry," she said. "I'm sorry, but I…" She didn't know what to say. She and the man whose eyes were as blue as hers stood there as if frozen for all time.

Jonah stood and laid a comforting arm around her waist. "It's a lot to think about. Perhaps we should come back later, either this afternoon or tomorrow."

Aunt Fay spoke up. "I think Nicholas and

Mary should go for a ride. Take her to the places the children loved to play when she was little," she told her husband. "She was young, but she seems to recall quite a bit. Let the past come back slowly, as naturally as possible."

Jonah gave Mary a little squeeze. "I think she's right."

The older woman touched Mary, lightly, quickly, on the arm. "I would love to have you for a daughter, but you need time to adjust to the idea. The Daltons tend to be just a bit overpowering," she said with a teasing smile at her husband. "We won't rush you, child. You mustn't worry."

Her words were a relief to Mary. She still didn't know what was expected of her, but she no longer felt stampeded into remembering a life here with the Daltons.

"Thank you." She faced Mr. Dalton. "I think a ride would be nice. It helps me think."

He nodded and led the way to the door.

"Shall I saddle a couple of mounts?" Jonah asked.

Mr. Dalton frowned at him. "The day I

can't handle my own saddle is the day I retire from riding."

"Right, sir."

Mary almost smiled when Mr. Dalton continued outside and Jonah brushed a finger across his forehead as if in relief, then grinned at her.

Later, when she followed Mr. Dalton across the pasture to a gate, she called to him, "I don't remember the ranch house or home pastures."

"There is a place," he began, then paused. "We used to have picnics there. Your mother—her name was Milly—would worry about you kids falling."

His glance when he said the name was penetrating, but for Mary it didn't conjure up a face or a hint of recognition. But then, she wouldn't have called her mother by her name, she decided as he rode ahead to open the gate at the far side of the meadow.

"Mother," she said under her breath. "Mom. Mommy."

Instinctively she knew that sounded right. For a three-year-old, it would have been.

"Daddy." She studied the lean, rangy

form of her companion as he leaned down and opened the latch on the gate. Was he the strong, laughing man who'd lifted her onto the saddle in front of him?

She pictured him as a younger man, his hair still dark like the other Dalton kin. No images of him and the child came to mind. Disappointed, she urged her horse into a trot and went through the open gate.

"Follow the road, then we'll take the trail up the ledge when we get to the cutoff," Mr. Dalton said, catching up.

She managed a smile. "I feel like Dorothy. Follow the yellow brick road, follow the yellow brick road," she said in a singsong. "She knew where her home was, but I...never have," she finished.

His manner was relaxed, she noted. There was patience and kindness in his eyes as he looked her over.

"I won't rush you, Mary," he said gruffly. "Now that you're home, we have all the time in the world."

"You seem so sure that I'm your lost daughter." The uncertainty she felt was reflected in the upward cadence of her voice on the last word.

He rode beside her, his expression introspective, for a couple of minutes. "I always thought I would know my own flesh and blood if we ever met again. For years after you…after Tink disappeared, my heart would hitch each time I spotted a dark-haired girl who was all legs and arms. As time went on, I gave up that dream. I thought it was the foolish longing of an old man."

The steady clop of the horses' hooves and, far away, the drone of an engine were steady, reassuring sounds as they continued along the road for another half mile.

Mr. Dalton pulled up at a trail heading uphill. "Then I ran into you."

"What if all this—" She gestured to the ranch and her strange memories of it. "What if it's some bizarre coincidence and I'm not Tink? What if I'm making it all up?"

"Are you?"

"I don't know. I can't tell what's real and what may be the longing of a foolish heart." She gave him a half smile as she rephrased his words and applied them to herself. "For an orphan, this would be a dream come true. Parents. Home. A big family, all happy to have you back. That's the problem. It's too much of a dream."

"There's a way to resolve it," he said. "My nephew Beau is a doctor. He could arrange a DNA test."

"Then we would know?"

He nodded.

"I think it would be better to do that before…before we…proceed."

"Then that's what we'll do," he said decisively. He clicked to his mount and led the way up a narrow trail through the mixed stand of pine, cedar and fir trees.

It was about an hour's journey to the bluff overlooking the valley. The tiny creek that she'd followed on the down slope from the road—and found the cabin—began its meandering path from a rocky depression cut into the west side of the hill she discovered when they dismounted and tied their horses next to it.

"This way," Mr. Dalton said.

She followed him onto the promontory that jutted out into the air. A huge flat-topped rock perched right at the edge. When the elder Dalton stepped on a smaller boulder, then hoisted himself onto the big rock, she did the same.

"This is wonderful," she said. "You can see the whole world from here."

"We call this the Devil's Dining Room. The boulder is his stool. This is his table we're standing on."

She laughed and was startled at the sound, it was so carefree. So happy. So unlike her.

Sobering, she approached the edge of the rock. She sat and let her legs dangle into space. It looked to be a thousand feet straight down. She felt no fear.

"There's our house," he said, pointing out the landmarks. "The stable and barn. The home paddock. The new hay shed with enough space in the middle to work with the cutting stock in the winter. That roof almost hidden in the trees belongs to Travis and Alison."

"Alison is Janis's sister. Janis is married to Keith, who is Jonah's partner at the Towbridge ranch."

"Right." He beamed as if she'd answered a particularly tricky question correctly.

"Travis and Trevor are twins. Zack, the lawman, is their older brother."

"Right again."

"Seth, the lawyer, and Beau, the doctor, are brothers to Roni, the only girl and the youngest of the Daltons."

He hesitated, then said softly, "Tink is the youngest by a few months. Roni was twenty-seven in May. Tink was twenty-seven in September."

"I won't be twenty-seven until March," she stated, as if this was proof she couldn't possibly be his daughter.

"A date given to you by the orphanage officials, if I'm not mistaken."

Her throat went tight. She nodded and gazed at the view, finding comfort in the peaceful scene to offset the turmoil within. If she was the lost child, then most of the *facts* about her existence—her age, birthday, place of birth, even her name—were false.

The man she and the authorities had assumed to be her father, wasn't. The man sitting beside her...

"When did you marry, uh, your present wife?" she asked.

"Two months ago. Call us Uncle Nick and Aunt Fay," he told her a trifle impatiently. "If you can't bring yourself to say Mother and Father."

She clasped her fingers over the jagged edge of the rock. "It's too new. I'm sorry. I can't."

He touched her shoulder, then withdrew. "I'm the one who should apologize. I'm rushing you and I know I shouldn't. It's just that time seems to be galloping past at a furious pace. I want my daughter back before it runs out on me."

"I understand."

It had been her experience that Fate could change its mind without a moment's notice and send a person on a new path in a new direction, heedless of that person's needs.

"The twins are cutting the last alfalfa hay of the season. See them in the field past the paddock?"

The plangent drone of the tractor reached her ears. "Yes. Mr. Dalton…Uncle Nick… how soon can we have the DNA test?"

"The sooner, the better. Let's head for the

house and call Beau. Perhaps we can go into town for lunch, then stop by the clinic."

Looking at the valley far below, Mary thought it looked like a postcard, the same as the peaks west of them had appeared to her the day she'd arrived in the Seven Devils Mountains. Nothing seemed real.

Except for one thing.

"Yes," she murmured, "let's go home."

But it wasn't the ranch lying like a paradise far below the Devil's Dining Room that she referred to.

She glanced toward the north before leaping down from the huge slab of stone. The red and beige cliffs weren't visible from there, but she knew where they were.

Somehow they'd become etched in her heart.

JONAH KEPT AN eye on Mary on the trip to town. Tension sat heavily on her slender shoulders. She hadn't uttered a word since they'd embarked on this new adventure—getting DNA samples from her and Uncle Nick.

Not that she ever said much. He smiled to himself at the truth in that thought.

"What will happen when the DNA test is returned and you are found to be the missing child?" he asked.

"I don't know."

"You and Uncle Nick didn't discuss the possibility?"

"No." She sighed a bit raggedly. "I don't suppose it will change anything. I'll go on working." She flicked him a keen-edged perusal. "Unless you decide you don't want me—"

She broke off, as if realizing how that sounded. Her face gave nothing away, but he sensed the undercurrents of emotion in her. Life had dealt her a hard hand to play. It made him angry on her behalf.

He managed a chuckle. "Why wouldn't I want you?" he demanded lightly. "You're the best wrangler we've ever had, and we'd starve without your skills in the kitchen."

He deliberately kept the focus on the ranch and away from the personal, but he was aware of her in ways he'd never been aware of other women. She was full of nuances and surprises, an equal mixture of passionate delight and hidden mysteries.

Her will to survive—and on her terms—
drew forth his admiration. Her stoic reserve
spoke to something primitive and protective
in him. And last but not least, her lithe wil-
lowy form stirred his blood.

"If word leaks out, there could be a big
to-do in the press. Missing heiress returns
and all that," she said.

"It'll be big news for a day or two, then
they'll be on to the next big thing."

They arrived at the town. He drove to the
Dalton lodge beside the lake and parked.
Uncle Nick and his wife stopped beside them.
They went inside and were shown to a table
in the back corner next to a window.

"While this doesn't command a view of
the higher peaks to the west, I always thought
this was the loveliest picture," Aunt Fay told
them when they were seated.

Jonah noted the waitress, the same one
who'd waited on them Friday, was staring at
Mary. He managed to bump against the girl
as he sat down and distract her. Frowning, he
ordered iced tea after the others did.

When the waitress hurried off, looking
back over her shoulder at Mary, he knew the

gossip would soon be spreading via the grapevine. He wondered if he should warn the others.

"That gal noticed your eyes," Uncle Nick said. "Everyone will be wondering who you are."

Mary smiled. "Until we get the results of the DNA test, we'll just let them stew. If it's positive, we can call a press conference and have our fifteen minutes of fame. If it's negative, we can tell the locals that I'm a distant cousin who wanted to meet the rest of the family. That should take care of the speculation."

Jonah relaxed a tad as her sense of humor asserted itself. She'd decided how to handle the situation.

"Let's order, then get over to Beau's clinic," Uncle Nick said. "I want to get this resolved."

During the meal, Jonah realized Uncle Nick's new wife was directing the conversation. She asked her husband question after question about raising the orphans. By the end of the meal, they had a well-rounded picture of life on the Seven Devils spread. He found himself chuckling several times.

To his right, he heard Mary's laughter at the antics of the Dalton gang, as the kids were called by the rest of the county residents.

"If anyone left a wagon or tractor out in the field anywhere near a barn on Halloween," the older man confided, "the kids would sneak over and, using ropes and pulleys, try to haul it onto the roof. They nearly succeeded with our hay wagon one year, but I caught them. Scared the bejesus out of 'em when I fired a blast of rock salt into the air."

"What about the girls?" Aunt Fay asked. "Did they join in?"

"Yep. Not even the threat of a whipping with a willow switch stopped Roni from taking part." His expression became somber. "Tink was gone by then. She and Roni had become best friends. After Tink disappeared, Roni tried to keep up with the boys. I think she was afraid of being left behind. She thought Tink had gotten lost, which is what we thought at first."

The laughter fled the foursome. Jonah noticed the tension had returned to the set of Mary's shoulders. Without thinking, he laid a hand on her neck and massaged the tight muscles.

It was only when he realized he was getting a keen scrutiny from Aunt Fay that he removed his hand. That woman saw way too much.

The problem with once having touched intimately, lovers then tended to touch casually thereafter, invading each other's private space. It was a tactic he'd successfully used in a TV commercial that had netted the advertising agency a cool thirty-million-dollar contract and his first million-dollar bonus.

When the food arrived, he realized he was hungry. It was nice to have something besides his usual soup or chili and sandwiches. Mary ate a few bites, then laid her fork down.

"You need to eat more," Uncle Nick scolded, frowning at her nearly full plate. "A good wind will blow you right over."

No emotion showed on her face as she explained. "I don't eat a lot at lunch. I'm usually working outside and just grab something quick. But the food here is delicious."

Jonah wondered at the times when she might not have had much to eat. If it came to a choice, she would buy food for that big horse of hers before she would for herself.

A funny pang went through him. He forced himself to study the view outside the window rather than stare at Mary and speculate on her life. He was aware of the older woman's quick glances and knew she'd caught the vibes between him and the long-lost daughter. He could hardly deny they existed.

If she was the missing child, and he was sure she was, where did that leave them? Nowhere. Exactly. Yeah, it was always a mistake to get mixed up with the hired help.

His cynical smile didn't ring quite true, not even to himself. Aunt Fay smiled unexpectedly and announced she for one wanted dessert. "Something really decadent," she said.

An hour later the two couples left the quiet lodge and headed into town. Jonah followed Uncle Nick's pickup to the gravel parking area next to a large Victorian mansion.

"We shouldn't be but a minute," Uncle Nick announced, getting out and opening Mary's door.

He took the wrangler's arm and ushered her inside the stately house that served as

Beau's medical clinic and Seth's law office. Beau and his family lived in the upper two stories while their new home at the lake was being built.

Feeling shut out, Jonah offered his arm to the new Mrs. Dalton. "Shall we tour the grounds?"

"It's unusually warm for September, isn't it?" the older woman remarked after a couple of minutes of admiring the flowers growing in beds scattered around the lawn.

"Yes. It's good because we're bringing the cattle in from the high country. It'll take a month to finish the roundup."

"Is Mary a good worker?"

"One of the best. Very conscientious."

She sniffed a late rose, then looked at him with a definite twinkle in her eyes. "Even if she isn't Nick's daughter, it would be good if she stayed in the area."

"Why?" he asked, keeping a neutral tone.

"She needs a place to belong. Everyone does. That doesn't mean one can't leave it and establish a new place, but people need ties if only to have a haven to return to."

He nodded. "Like me. I saw the rest of the

world and decided this was the best place to be."

She eyed him as if she would ask more, but she continued their walk around the garden. "The girl belongs to Nick," she said bluntly. "He'll want her to live in his house, at least for a while. It'll be best for her, too. She'll need to explore her new identity and discover who she is…who she really is…without complications."

He recognized a warning when he heard one. "I won't stand in her way."

"Good."

When Uncle Nick and Mary reappeared, Jonah took a good look at them. They were as alike as a father and daughter could be. Mary had said the orphans made up stories about their families. He wondered if she'd like the one she was about to acquire.

"Beau said the lab promised to hurry the results," the older man told them, smiling in a pleased fashion.

Aunt Fay rolled her eyes. "That certainly surprises us."

Their laughter died into awkward silence when they stood beside the trucks.

"You can stay at our place while we wait," Uncle Nick said to Mary.

She glanced at Jonah, then the elder Dalton. Her smile was apologetic. "I have a job to do. My boss is pretty strict about getting things done on time."

Jonah pretended to give her a cuff on the arm. "That's right," he said. "She's the new wrangler. She has to take care of the stock before dark."

Disappointment flashed into blue eyes, but the old man nodded. "Well, I'm sure we'll know something about the test soon, then we can decide what to do."

After he and Mary were on their way back to the Towbridge ranch, enveloped in their usual cloud of silence, he said, "If the results are positive, I won't hold you to the job. Uncle Nick will want you to move over there so you and the family can get to know each other."

"You sound pretty certain about my future."

"Honey, it's as plain as the nose on your face. Also your hair and eyes and build," he added, keeping a light tone.

Her throat moved as she swallowed, then

nodded. "Let's go home. I want to work with Attila before evening chores. Unless you need me for something else. I noticed the firewood you cut. Should I move it to the lodge for this winter?"

"We'll load it on the hay wagon, then store it on the porch next to the side door of the great room. Tomorrow we'll have to head up the trail. Keith has more cattle for us to bring down."

Her smile bloomed. "I liked staying at the cabin."

"I think you would make a great hermit," he told her, "but we should be able to get to the high meadow and back before dark."

At the ranch headquarters, he had to deal with three families who'd decided to take advantage of the weather and get in one last camping trip. Mary headed toward the pasture where Attila was grazing.

After taking the camping fees and writing out receipts, then, concealing impatience, helping the campers in the store, he was detained by the telephone and had to take several calls, including one from his partner, Keith.

Finally as twilight swept the land, he headed for the paddock where Mary coaxed the stallion through his gaits using a lunge line. Leaning against the fence post, he observed the quiet way she handled the horse.

When the workout was done, she released the rope and came over to where Jonah stood. The stallion followed at her heels like an adoring canine, then laid his head on her shoulder and lipped her ear, which made her laugh and shoo him away.

"He's letting me know you belong to him," Jonah told her.

Her quick glance was amused but wary. As usual.

"You're going to have a lot of demands made on you during the foreseeable future."

She nodded, stuck her hands into her back pockets and gazed at the mountains to the west. The sun was already low behind them. The shadows cast by the trees were velvety in texture, blurring together in the pattern of darkness.

"I checked the stock and the fences," she said. "The mineral block was nearly gone. I put out another one."

She clearly didn't want to discuss the situation. Tough. They had to face certain things.

"Good." He couldn't resist touching her hair and smoothing the tendrils that blew around her face. "I won't add to those demands," he said, feeling the slight stiffening of her shoulders as he continued his line of thought. "Your work here won't be a problem. If you need time off to take care of other matters, it's okay."

"Thanks," she said without looking at him.

"There'll be time later to explore how things stand between us."

She shrugged.

"Dammit, Mary, look at me!" He controlled his temper as she swung around to face him, her beautiful face closed and remote. He wanted to shake her, but common sense prevailed. She'd assumed her protective cloak of indifference, so he knew he was hitting close to her heart.

"Don't worry about last night," she said. "It was nothing. I don't expect anything from you because of it."

He frowned at the fence that stood between

them, at the stallion who stayed at her side and kept a baleful eye on him.

"Let's go inside," he said.

He walked along the fence to the gate and opened it after she turned the stallion into the pasture once more. They went to the house in silence. The aroma of a baking chicken filled the air when they went inside. He realized she'd put a meal on before she went outside. He felt guilty for not thinking of it himself.

"I'd like to shower before eating."

He nodded and watched her stride down the corridor in long, graceful steps. His body tightened as he thought of joining her.

"Back off," he warned his libido. She had enough to think about without the confusing impact of desire between them. He had some thinking of his own to do before this drama played itself out.

Chapter Eleven

Saturday of the next week dawned sunny but cooler than the previous days. Only three more days and the month would be over, Mary mused as she headed for the pasture. Eleven days and there was still no word on the DNA test.

Grimacing, she tossed a bareback pad on a cowpony and rode across the meadow and back. After exercising all six of the riding stock, she cornered the mules and worked with them on a lead rope for a few minutes, then she let all the animals return to grazing on the dry grass of the field.

Due to her attention to the other animals, Attila sulked beside the fence and wouldn't look at her when she went over to check his leg.

"Lift," she said, grasping his ankle.

He shifted his weight and let her pick up his hoof and flex it back and forth. He also lifted her hat.

"Give me that," she scolded when she finished with his leg. She put the hat on and pulled the brim low over her forehead so it wouldn't blow off.

A breeze was kicking up dust along the road. She glanced toward the west, but there were no threatening clouds on the horizon. Close by, a cow also stared into the distance and bellowed loudly for no reason that Mary could determine.

Jonah had been right about the mama cows. After two days, or three for a couple of the stubborn ones, they'd quit calling for their calves and resumed grazing.

Too bad it wasn't as easy for humans.

Leaving the stock after one last visual sweep, she returned to the house. Seeing that Jonah had split and loaded another stack of logs on the wagon, she carried the wood up the steps of the side porch and stored it with the growing pile near the door. They could easily burn two or three cords a month in the fireplace, he'd said.

The fireplace was mainly a backup to the furnace, but it was also used when they had guests. The hunters liked to sit around the hearth and recount the day's adventures, which, according to Jonah, grew more daring as the evening grew longer.

It took thirty minutes to unload the wagon. Panting lightly, Mary sat on the porch railing and rested before going inside to shower.

Recounting the days, she realized she'd been at the ranch/camping/hunting resort for nearly a month. All day yesterday and today she'd expected a call from the Daltons advising her that she wasn't the missing Tink.

For some reason it was easier to think she wasn't the child than to contemplate what would happen if she was.

In the orphanage, life had been easier if the kids didn't get their hopes up too high. She'd listened to more than one child sobbing in the night when the couple who'd taken them out for a day had decided not to adopt. The pain of rejection burned deep into the soul.

"Dinner is ready," Jonah said from the open door leading to the great room.

Glancing at his tall masculine form, she

was reminded of the solid strength of him, the special way he'd made her feel that involved more than passion, although that had been wonderful. He would make a good husband—steadfast, dependable, honorable, loving…

"Mary?"

She loved his voice. The depth of it. The quiet in it, as if she'd find an oasis in his arms.

"Mary," he said again, but this time the timbre had changed, becoming deeper, softer…sensuous, as if he'd recognized the longing in her.

Peace and pleasure. Safety. Excitement. He was all those things. She moved instinctively toward him.

His eyes darkened. He held a hand out, waiting to receive her, to take her into his arms. She stopped no more than an inch from him.

Sudden laughter caused her heart to do a giant leap. "Is someone here?" she asked, stepping back. "The Daltons…"

"Hikers for the weekend, that's all."

She nodded, not sure whether she felt relieved or disappointed. "Do you need some help?"

"No. Go take your shower and relax." He stood aside so she could enter, his gaze restlessly roaming her face.

After shucking her boots, she carried them upstairs to her room, then ducked into the shower and quickly cleaned up. Dressed in sweats, she padded down to the kitchen.

Jonah was filling a wooden bowl with crackers. A platter of various types of cheese and cut vegetables was already on the counter. When she tasted the stew and added a bit more garlic and pepper, he gave her a quick smile.

He seemed perfectly at ease, but she was nervous around him. Since the tension-filled lunch and DNA test with the Daltons, she and Jonah had staged an odd dance, one in which they very carefully made sure they didn't touch each other in any way.

But the hunger was there, simmering like a witch's brew of trouble between them. Each night she had to fight it as she lay alone in her bed. Each morning she had to face him and see in his eyes the same restlessness that was in hers.

She helped him carry the food into the dining room where four couples sat and chatted over glasses of wine. She glanced at her boss in question.

"They brought their own," he murmured.

After making sure the guests had everything they needed, she and Jonah prepared their own plates. He gestured for her to follow him. They went through the office into the sunroom.

Two chairs flanked a small, round oak table in one corner. They settled there and ignored the large bed where they'd shared bliss, then peace, for a few hours.

"Be right back," he said.

He returned in a couple of minutes with two glasses of nonfat milk. She smiled her thanks.

"You don't carry wine or beer in the store," she said after quelling the hunger pangs by eating half the stew. She studied his face in the soft glow of the setting sun.

"No. It isn't something I like to have

around." His smile was rueful. "I suppose you want to know why."

"I'd wondered."

"My father was an alcoholic. Not at first, not during my early years. It was a gradual thing. When I went off to college on a scholarship, my mother decided she'd had enough. They divorced during my freshman year."

For some reason, she'd assumed his father was dead. Perhaps because he hadn't mentioned him before now that she could recall.

"That must have been disturbing, to come home and find the family you'd left didn't exist anymore. Where is your father now?" she asked.

"Retired and living in southern California. He was a firefighter with the National Park Service. Now he's a consultant for several counties on wildfire prevention."

"Neither of your parents remarried?"

"My father has. My stepmother was a widow. She told him he had to give up the booze if he wanted her."

"Did he?"

Jonah nodded. "At first I resented the fact that he didn't do that for my mother. Later,

I realized she didn't give him a choice. She told him to leave. I think that was a mistake. People have to be upfront about their expectations."

She thought this over. "Is there a lesson for me in this?"

He gave her a brief smile. "I like my stepmother. She and my father are happy. So is my mom. She has plenty of family, so she's not lonely. People can make new family connections."

While considering all this information, Mary finished the meal and drank down the last drops of milk. "Have you heard anything about the DNA test?" she asked, drawing her own conclusions about family connections.

"No. Beau will call the moment he hears. Since the lab is in Boise and it's the only one in this part of the state that can run the test, it'll probably be another week before the results are in."

She exhaled heavily, feeling like a condemned person who'd gotten a reprieve from the governor.

"It's odd to meet someone who's reluctant to become an heiress," Jonah murmured.

"It isn't that," she said, managing a wry smile and shrugging off the odd doldrums. "It's not knowing what comes next that bothers me."

"You'll go live with your father and be the pampered daughter of the Dalton clan. You can go to college and become anything you want. You can pursue your dream of making the Olympics. Your cousins will all pitch in to help."

Their eyes met. Silken threads arced between them as awareness grew too strong to be ignored. Finally he gave a snort of ironic laughter as if amused with their predicament, then looked away.

She continued to study him as he swallowed the last bite of stew, then laid the spoon aside and finished off the milk.

The truth came to her slowly but as surely as the rising of the sun. She didn't want a new life. She didn't want to live somewhere else.

"I like it here." She heard the stubborn undercurrent in her voice. "I've always earned my own way."

"You're independent. The Daltons will

surely understand that attitude. It's a family characteristic."

"Are you insulting me and my, uh, possible family?" she demanded, trying to substitute a lighter mood for the restless unhappiness she felt. She didn't know what was wrong with her, but it confused her as much as the new direction her life seemed to be taking.

He glanced at her in surprise, then, with a smile playing at the corners of his mouth, stroked the sensitive skin under her chin. "Atta girl," he said.

Pleasure rushed through her at the approval in his eyes. It was such an odd feeling that it took her a moment to realize what it was.

MIDNIGHT. MARY STARED at the clock to make sure it was running. The minute hand ticked off another sixty seconds.

Outside, the night was black and silver as a distant moon scattered its argentine light over the land. From far, far away came the lonely howl of a coyote seeking another of its kind.

She waited for an answer, but none came.

Unable to settle, she finally pulled on thick socks, unlocked her door and slipped into the hallway. Every nerve sizzled at a noise, then she realized the sound was the snoring of a guest in the room opposite hers.

Exasperated with her nervy jumps and starts, she went down the steps, intending to go to the kitchen for a cup of hot milk.

"Can't sleep?" a masculine voice asked.

She wasn't surprised to find Jonah standing at the back door and gazing at the nightscape as she'd been doing from her window for the past hour. "No."

Somehow a decision was made, one she didn't even know she'd been contemplating. She went to his side and stood there for a few seconds, then she sighed and leaned against him.

His arm encircled her waist, bringing that strange blend of comfort and excitement he induced in her.

She wrapped both arms around him and linked her hands together, letting them rest against his hip. Her head went to the groove of his shoulder like a nestling finding its home.

After a second he released a heavy breath and laid his cheek against the top of her head.

"My control isn't too dependable at the present."

"Neither is mine."

There was a pause, then he chuckled. "Must you be so damned honest?"

She rolled her head so she could look up into his eyes. His mouth was only inches away. If she but lifted her head a tiny bit, their lips would touch.

"You're making me desperate," he muttered, the laughter still there but muted now.

"That's how I feel."

He peered out at the night once more. "You have reason to feel that way. Your life is going through a pretty drastic change. Again."

Some subconscious fear made her tighten her hold around him, as if she might be snatched away at any moment.

"What if…what if I don't want to go?"

His hand caressed through her hair, loosening the braid until it flowed free around her shoulders. "You have to."

The words hurt. She dropped her arms and pushed back. He refused to let her go. Instead he looped both his arms around her and held her close.

"You're going to have a new life to explore. Once you've done that, then if you want to come back here, you can." He gave a faint snort of amusement. "In the meantime I'll be like that ol' coyote out there, lonesome and peevish, howling at the moon and not getting a response."

The stiffness eased out of her shoulders and she leaned into him once more. "You might hear me howling back," she murmured.

He turned fully toward her. The hardness of his body told her of his desire. The gentleness of his touch told her of his concern.

"You'll be too busy to be lonely," he assured her. "Uncle Nick will put you to work. He doesn't believe in idle hands, or so his nephews say. When he sees how good you are with animals, he'll probably want to start a line of hunters from your stallion."

She managed a laugh. "I'd like that." After a moment, she added, "I don't think Attila will be able to compete in the future. There's an instability in his ankle that wasn't noticeable before the injury."

"When was he hurt?"

"The first week in June."

Jonah experienced a need to reassure her. "So it's been a little over three months. Sometimes pulled tendons can take a year to heal."

"True."

He heard the stoic resolve in the word. If her horse didn't recover, she would take care of him the rest of his life, no matter what the cost to her. And no one, including the dun, would know what dreams she'd given up.

Jonah clenched his teeth as a wide range of emotions ran through him. He'd never met anyone who could make him feel both angry and tender. Angry because of her stubborn independence. Tender because he had an inkling of what it cost for her to achieve it.

When she stirred against him, he gently set her away from him, trying to ignore the clamor of protest that rose inside him. "You'd better go to bed, wrangler. Tomorrow will be a busy day."

She nodded but didn't move. The wall sconces backlighted her slender figure, giving her a mythical, mysterious aura. Her eyes seemed as dark as the night sky in the dim light.

He inhaled sharply. "Then stay," he said

in a near whisper and gathered her into his arms once more.

Hunger raged through his blood. He needed the taste of her, the woman-essence of her. He needed the completion of making deep intimate love with her.

A groan was wrung from him as she pressed closer, her arms going around his neck, her fingers into his hair. His blood thickened as the embrace deepened. The kiss involved lips and teeth and tongue. Each of them tasted and nipped and demanded more from the other.

"I could take you right here," he murmured. "Standing. Sitting. Lying on a table. It doesn't matter. Nothing does when I hold you."

"It's strange to feel this way."

She held his face between her palms and studied him with that worried little frown that was all she usually allowed the world to see when she was troubled.

He kissed the end of her nose. "Not so strange. Once having known this kind of bliss, it's hard to give it up."

"Yes, but I've never felt like this, as if there's a river flooding through me, taking sense and caution with it. Why? Where did it come from?"

The bewilderment was genuine, he realized. What's more, he even understood it. "It's that old man-woman thing. People have been trying to figure it out since Adam and Eve."

She slid her hands down his throat and onto his chest. When she found the end of his sweatshirt, she slipped her hands under the edge and ran them up his torso. She kissed each inch of flesh as she exposed it. Her tongue teased his nipples until they stood at attention.

"Come on," he ordered huskily. "There's only so much a man can take."

"But there's so much more," she teased.

Arm in arm, they went to the sunroom and shucked their clothing, their eyes on each other as they did.

He caught her hands and held them out to each side so he could gaze his fill of her alluring curves in the moonlight.

Her breasts were high, the tips already tightly budded, waiting for his kisses. He bent forward and laved them with quick, passionate touches of his lips and tongue.

A drum roll of passion went through him like hot quicksilver. He released her hands and slid his along her sides, moving upward. He could feel the graceful curve of her ribs through the taut flesh covering them.

Exploring downward, he found the lines of her waist and hips to be sweetly feminine. Dropping to one knee, he nuzzled his face against her abdomen and felt the muscles contract as her breath quickened.

With leisurely intent, he took pleasure in the smoothness of her skin, the downy feel of her Venus mound and the intimate warmth of her womanly body.

Her hands caressed through his hair. "My knees are getting weak," she warned.

"Hold on to me. I'm not through with you yet." He nipped at her thigh. "I want you to melt."

She laughed softly. "I want the same from you."

"No," he corrected. "You don't want me to melt."

He refused to let her go or to let up on the

passion until he felt her trembling, then he took pity on her and let her fall back on the bed. He joined her and rolled them to the center of the king-size mattress.

Their arms and legs tangled like rose vines twining around each other. When her gasps and little cries drove him beyond endurance, he took care of protection. His hands were shaking, he was that desperate for her.

Yet when they merged into one, he suddenly found himself satisfied to stay that way and simply rest for a moment.

She would have none of it.

To his surprised pleasure, she became the aggressor. When she sought the top position, he let her have her way.

"Now I'm the one who's melting," he managed to say, laughing at their mutual hunger and the combination of strength and weakness it drew from both of them. He realized he'd never been with a woman who so exactly matched him in bed and out, in their hopes and dreams and ambitions.

All his thoughts shattered as she gasped his name on a low, compelling moan. His control frayed and disappeared as they moved together on the tidal wave of completion.

"Honey, honey, honey," he murmured, shaken by the depth, the satisfaction he felt.

When they rested side by side, he smoothed her sexy, luxurious mass of hair away from her face. Finding moisture at her temples, he traced it to the corner of her eye.

"Mary?" he questioned. When she didn't answer, he asked, "What's wrong?"

"Nothing," she said.

"You're crying over nothing?" He kept his tone gentle, but he was worried. After what they'd shared, tears were the last thing he would have expected.

"Because it was so good," she finally murmured. "Because good things don't last."

The implication that their lovemaking was a fleeting pleasure angered him for some reason. He didn't feel up to examining why at the moment. "Maybe some do," he argued.

She shook her head. He caught the brief, sad flash of her smile, then she turned and cupped her body into his and settled into sleep.

He laid a protective arm across her waist

and pressed his face into the sweet warmth of her hair. They needed to talk, but not now. For the present, he'd take the bliss.

MARY WOKE SLOWLY. A beam of light fell to the floor from a gap between two curtain panels. She stretched, then spread her arm over the wide bed. She was alone.

Her sweats were neatly folded on a chair, her socks on top of the pile. She slipped the clothing on, then left the sun room. From the clock in the office, she was shocked to find the morning less than two hours from being over.

Ten-twenty. She couldn't remember a time when she'd slept this late, no matter what hour she'd gone to bed.

The hum of electricity along her nerves invoked the magic of the night and the peace she'd found with Jonah. She wanted to see him. The need was too strong to ignore.

Rushing up the steps, she showered, dressed and braided her hair as quickly as her suddenly clumsy fingers would allow. Noticing the open doors as she headed downstairs, she wondered where everyone was.

No one was in the kitchen, but the big urn held coffee. She poured a cup and checked the windows for signs of activity down at the stables and pasture. Spotting Attila and one of the mares, she realized the other horses were gone.

Ah, Jonah must have taken the visitors on a trail ride.

She scowled at the disappointment that pinged through her, then surprised herself by laughing. Her spirits were soaring and nothing could dampen that fact.

Deciding a treat was in order, she squeezed off a chunk of sourdough from the bowl in the refrigerator, stirred in the flour, sugar, salt and butter for making cinnamon rolls and set the mixture aside to rise.

After breakfast, she checked on Attila. His limp wasn't worse, but neither did it seem to be getting better. Even that didn't daunt her for long. Whatever happened, she could handle it. She returned to the house.

"Hello," a man called from the great room.

Her heart speeded up, but it was a camper wanting some groceries. He was frowning when she entered the store.

"This coffee costs a fortune," he complained, holding up a one-pound can.

"That's because we have to buy it retail in town. Our turnover isn't great enough for a wholesale distributor to come out here."

"Huh," he said, clearly not caring about the reasons.

She had no trouble maintaining a smile. When he'd gathered the items he needed, she added them up and made change for him. Several people must have been in that morning for there was quite a bit of cash.

Once the man left, she eyed the cash box, then removed all the money except for the coins, a five-dollar bill and four ones. After counting up almost a hundred dollars, she placed the money in an envelope and tucked it in a drawer in the office.

Retracing her steps, she went into the kitchen, washed her hands and kneaded the dough until it felt right. She rolled it out, brushed it with melted butter and generously coated it with cinnamon sugar, then rolled the dough up and cut it into half-inch slices. In a square baking pan, she added more butter and brown sugar, then placed the rolls on top and set it aside to rise once more.

Searching through the freezer, she found a roast and thawed it in the microwave oven and put it on to bake. She felt very domestic as she worked. And happy.

It was a sobering thought. Happiness was more often a thing remembered than experienced.

The sunshine beckoned, and she went outside. Sitting on the top step of the porch, she contemplated her mood. Whatever the future held, she would always consider the month she'd spent here as special.

Peering at the mountains surrounding the area, she recalled that the name Seven Devils had intrigued her when she'd first heard it. Her feelings had been mixed upon actually arriving. There'd been that odd uneasiness, the troubling scenes that had come to her and the funny taunt of the other children. She hadn't been able to tell if those were memories or the mixed up dreams of a lonely child.

And then there was Jonah.

The sound of his name was like a song playing over and over inside her. A happy song.

She was still smiling when he and the guests returned to the home place. She rose and headed down the path. At the stable, the couples told her what a good time they'd had. They were thrilled that they'd seen a black bear.

"Only it was more tan that black," one of the women said.

"And as big as a grizzly," the other added. "Jonah said the horses could outrun a bear. I'm glad we didn't have to find that out."

Jonah gave Mary a wink when she glanced at him. Her heart lurched, then righted itself and beat like crazy. She hadn't felt this way since she was eighteen and had believed in love and all that.

Not that she was in love. She wasn't.

A tremor shook through her like a small earthquake, as if something inside her wanted to argue the point. She quickly seized the reins. "I'll take care of the stock."

"Man, I'm starved. What is that delicious smell?"

Mary sniffed. The aroma of roasting meat came to her on the breeze. "I put on a roast earlier. The vegetables are ready to go in the pan with it. Lunch should be ready in an hour after that." She glanced at her watch. It was almost one. "I, uh, I slept late this morning."

"Technically it's your day off," Jonah said, "so you don't have to do anything. I'm the one who forgot to put something in to cook before we hit the trail this morning. Let's see if we can't rustle up a snack to tide us over."

Mary was grateful that he covered for her ridiculous attack of embarrassment at admitting she'd overslept. His gaze lingered on her for a second longer before he followed the guests to the lodge. A smile hovered on his mouth.

She removed and stored the tack, checked hooves, then turned the horses into the pasture. They went as a group to the watering trough and noisily drank their fill. Attila and the mare came over and exchanged noisy greetings. The two mules hee-hawed in welcome, then resumed eating. Soon the horses joined them. The scene was utterly peaceful.

Taking a deep breath of the fall air, Mary headed for the kitchen to finish the roast and put the rolls in to bake. The temperature had dropped to forty degrees last night, but today the sun was shining, its warmth caressing her head and shoulders as she walked up the path. The air seemed filled with magic, and every blade of grass was golden.

Almost heaven.

She smiled at the foolish thought, but it wouldn't budge from her mind. This rugged land might not be paradise, but it was surely close.

"Hi, you're just in time," Jonah said when she entered the kitchen. "I've put potatoes, carrots and onions in the roasting pan. Does it need anything else?"

"No, that should do it." She washed up and removed the dish towel from the pan of rolls. "These are ready to go in the oven, too."

"You have been busy," he murmured, holding the oven door open so she could slide the pan inside. "It's nice to come home to—"

She made room for the rolls beside the roasting pan while she waited for his next words.

"To a hot meal and cinnamon rolls," he concluded. "And a beautiful woman," he added in a husky whisper.

He closed the oven.

From upstairs, she could hear the laughter of the couples as they called to each other from their rooms. The shower came on. They were apparently cleaning up before lunch.

Neither she nor Jonah moved for a couple of seconds. She felt as if her feet were rooted to the spot. She couldn't step closer to him. She couldn't step away.

He touched her shoulder, turning her to face him. "The moment I've been waiting for," he said.

His smile was like the sun, a warm, visual caress that dipped right inside and circled around her whole body. She couldn't help but smile, too.

He gazed into her eyes, then lowered his head. Just before their lips touched, he closed his eyes. So did she.

The kiss was sweet and exactly what she was hungry for. Like a greedy child, she pressed forward, wanting more.

His hands roamed her back, stopping briefly at her hips as if taking her measurement. He opened his stance and pulled her closer until she could feel every curve and hard plane of his masculine body. She realized she wanted more.

"Hey!" someone shouted, a warning in the word.

There was the sound of a door slamming, then running steps. She heard the roar of an engine and spotted a truck zooming past the door as she and Jonah dashed toward the front to see what was going on.

Zack Dalton stood on the porch. "I should shoot out his tires," he said in disgust.

"What's going on?" Jonah asked.

"A burglary. The guy went through your cash box. I didn't notice him until I was half-way across the room and heard a racket in the store. He was trying to force a drawer open. When he saw me, he took off."

Jonah went into the store. The cash box was open and held only coins. "There's nothing in the drawer. I left the cash in the box on the counter so people could make their own change."

"A cigar box," Zack said ruefully. "That would certainly deter a thief. How much money did he get?"

Jonah shrugged. "I have no idea."

"Not much," Mary told them. "There was almost a hundred dollars when I checked out one of the campers this morning. I didn't like his attitude, so I put the money in an envelope and hid it in the office. I left a five and four ones, plus the coins, in the box." She went to the office and returned with the envelope. She handed it to Jonah.

Both men gave her an approving smile. "Good thinking," the lawman said. "Unless you want to press charges, I won't call in an APB on the man," he said to Jonah.

"Nah, it's not worth it. What brings you out our way?" Jonah asked.

"I talked to Beau this morning."

Mary stiffened as a tangle of emotions played havoc with her innermost being. Jonah laid a hand on her shoulder as if to steady her for the news.

Zack glanced at him, then her. He smiled. "Welcome home, Tink."

Chapter Twelve

Zack explained that the lab had been so swamped with work they hadn't been able to get to any procedures that weren't an emergency, so Beau had called in a couple of favors. A friend had agreed to finish the work over the weekend. He'd phoned Beau little more than an hour ago with the good news. "Beau then called me. I volunteered to tell you," he ended.

"There's no doubt about it?" Jonah asked.

"Well, Beau said the lab tech said the odds were 914,000,000 to one that she's a Dalton and a direct descendant of Uncle Nick's. That sounded pretty conclusive to me."

"Does Mr. Dalton know?" Mary asked.

Zack checked his watch. "Beau and his family should be arriving at the ranch about now. He wanted to be there in case Uncle Nick had another spell with his heart."

Mary pressed a hand to her middle as the world tossed like a ship on a stormy sea. "W-what should I do?"

Her newly found cousin gave her a sympathetic smile. "Naturally he'll want to see you as soon as possible. Then, well, I guess that's up to the two of you."

She turned to Jonah. He moved a step away and dropped his hand from her shoulder. She missed the warmth.

"You have to go," he told her. "You can come back for your clothing and personal things later."

Like a dash of cold water to the face, she snapped out of the panicky abyss of emotion. He'd stated what she knew to be true. She was no longer Mary McHale, cowgirl and Olympic hopeful. She was Theresa Ann Dalton. Tink.

"You can ride over with me," Zack said. "I'll bring you back when everything's worked out."

"Zack, when we were children, do you remember this? 'Tinkerbell, Tinkerbell, got in trouble and went to jail,'" she repeated the taunt, her eyes glued to his.

A smile of surprise lit his face. "Of course. Trevor made it up one time when you were being punished for some infraction of the rules. It stuck. After that, all of us boys teased you unmercifully when you got in trouble. Roni was usually in hot water with you."

"I thought I was going insane, hearing children's voices and their laughter. And the taunt."

"No, that was true. Not very nice, but we were boys. I hope you'll forgive us."

He sounded so sincere Mary found herself nodding as if taking the past episodes seriously. "There's nothing to forgive. I hope Roni and I gave as good as we got?"

"Yep. You two knew how to push our buttons, then you told on us if we threatened retaliation."

Mary realized how odd it was to exchange stories of the past with someone who actually knew her past. She glanced at Jonah and found him observing with casual interest.

He'd moved away from them, clearly marking himself as the odd man out in this strange tableau.

A funny pang hit her heart. "Jonah…" She wasn't sure what to say to him.

"Go with Zack," he said. "Take a change of clothing. Your family will expect you to spend the night."

For the tiniest space of time between one blink of her eyes and another, she felt the familiar sense of abandonment wash over her. Before she could give in to weakness and demand that he come with her, she nodded and started for the stairs.

"I'm surprised Uncle Nick hasn't called and wanted to know what's holding us up," she heard Zack say to Jonah.

"Tell him not to rush her. She's learned the hard way not to trust people. Give her time to adjust."

"Don't worry. Aunt Fay will keep the whole gang in check, including Uncle Nick. She's the only member of the family who's not afraid of his tongue."

Mary ran lightly up the steps as the two men chuckled, then chatted about the weather and the fall cattle count. Her fingers trembled while she packed a small nylon duffel with toiletries, the old sweat suit she slept in and a change of clothing. She kept her work boots on, but stuck her beige shoes in the bag just in case.

Just in case of what, she hadn't a clue.

Pausing before the wall mirror mounted over a chest, she stared at her image as if seeking insight on how she might be different now that she was somebody else.

Again a swirl of emotion spiraled off to some deep, secret place. "Who are you?" she whispered to the child who stared back at her. "Who am I?"

Downstairs, she found the men sitting on the front porch. "I'm ready," she said and inhaled deeply, drawing courage from the quiet ambiance of the place. The delicious scent of cinnamon filled her head. "The rolls!"

Dropping her bag, she raced for the kitchen just in time to rescue the treat. Setting the pan aside, she checked the veggies lining the roasting pan. "Lunch is ready," she said to Jonah when he appeared.

"You haven't eaten," he reminded her.

"I'm not very hungry."

"There'll be plenty left over at the other place. Aunt Fay and Lyric cook enough for a small army since they never know who's going to show up for a meal."

"Well, I'm ready as I'll ever be," Mary told the men, replacing the mitts in a drawer after turning off the oven.

"Take the rolls," Jonah said.

She shook her head. "They're for our guests."

He gave Zack an exasperated glance. "I knew she was a Dalton. She's as stubborn as any of you."

"Come on, cuz. We don't have to stay here and listen to these feeble insults. We can go over to Uncle Nick's and be insulted by experts."

She followed the lawman to his patrol SUV. Jonah held the door, then stored her bag in the backseat, which was fenced off from the front. "I've only ridden in a police car once before," she told the men as she buckled up. "It's sort of worrying, like I might be a prisoner and won't know it until I'm thrown in jail."

"Buck up," Jonah advised. "You're the cherished daughter of a local land baron, a legend in his own time and all that. Relax and enjoy your new life."

But when Zack drove around the circular driveway and headed toward the county road, she couldn't help but look back. Jonah stood on the porch. He waved.

She waved, too, then faced the front.

"Something going on between you two?" Zack asked.

For some reason the question didn't seem intrusive. She had a zillion questions about her new family. They probably had a zillion about her.

"Jonah has been very kind," she said, side-stepping the real issue. "He's…a very good boss."

They rode in silence for a while. Her cousin briefly studied her when he stopped before turning onto the gravel road that would take them to the other ranch. His expression was grave.

"Uncle Nick will need you to stay with him for a few weeks at least. He's missed out on twenty-three years of your life. It'll take some time to catch up."

She focused on one of many things that bothered her. "I don't know what to call him."

Zack frowned. "That would be a problem for me, too." He shrugged. "Don't call him anything until something comes naturally. Give yourself time to adjust. I'm sure Aunt Fay has given the same advice to him."

"She's my stepmother. I don't know what to call her, either," Mary admitted.

"Yeah, and from there, it gets complicated," he said with a generous dollop of irony. "Parents, cousins, in-laws. I was born into it… mmm, come to think of it, so were you."

"But I don't remember it, not much, at any rate." She sighed. "I'll take it one day at a time."

"Atta girl," he said with an understanding smile.

Jonah had said that to her. She suddenly missed him, more than she'd ever missed anyone, whether in real life or in her imagination. She resolutely set her face forward as they drove under the entrance logs of the Seven Devils ranch.

It took a minute before she realized she

was counting the people who gathered on the porch to await their arrival.

The family patriarch, his wife, Trevor and Lyric, Beau and his wife and son. Seven of them.

"Seven," she said, then was surprised at the sound of her voice.

"With the two of us, that'll make nine," Zack said with a keen glance at her as if he'd read her mind. "Maybe we're not devils, after all."

Mary barely smiled at his quip, then she opened the door and slid down from the SUV until her feet touched solid ground. Her eyes met those of the Dalton patriarch.

Her father.

She had to open her mouth to breathe. Like the night Cal had abandoned her, fear rioted through her, pinning her to the spot. This was family, she reminded herself. Her real family.

"Come on," Zack said with gruff kindness. He took her arm and led her to the group on the porch. "Here's Tink," he announced. "Home at last."

The boy who stood between Beau and his nurse-wife stepped forward. "Dad says you're my new cousin." He looked Mary over with obvious interest.

Glad of the distraction, she stooped and held out her hand. They shook solemnly. "I've never been a cousin before. You'll have to give me some hints on what to do."

"Sure," he said with the confidence of a child who knew his place in the family.

Mary stood and looked at her father. His smile was a bit unsteady. Like hers. She didn't know what to do.

Mrs. Dalton broke up the awkward moment. "We've prepared the rose room for you, Mary. Zack, take her bag in there. Lyric, put the rolls in the oven to brown. We'll eat first, then talk later."

Mary followed Zack into the house and down the hall. He placed her bag in the bedroom at the end of the wing. "You have your own bath," he said. "That's the closet."

He pointed to a second door in the large room decorated with pink roses on the wallpaper and embroidered on the bed coverlet. It was a pretty room, feminine and cozy. Zack nodded to her, exited and closed the door as if he knew she needed privacy at this moment.

Spotting a doll in a little stroller next to a bureau on the other side of the bed, she went to it. Lifting the doll, she stared into its lovely, vacuous eyes for a long minute.

The floor shifted and heaved under her feet. She sat down abruptly, her back to the wall and propped the doll on her knees. "I know you," she murmured. "You're Wendy. I wanted to be Tinkerbell and go around sprinkling fairy dust on people so they could fly."

The earth seemed to tremble once more under her. She closed her eyes and pressed the doll to her breast. The laughter of children came to her…a happy sound…carefree…then a deeper sound…a man's voice…his chuckle as he lifted a child onto the saddle…

Mary knew that voice, that man.

She rose, laid the doll gently into the stroller and left the pleasant room. Silence prevailed when she walked into the living room. Her eyes went to the elder Dalton.

"There was once a strong, laughing man," she told him. "He used to lift me onto the saddle in front of him. Is that a memory or a dream?"

He stood and took two steps toward her, then stopped. "A memory."

"You were that man." It was no longer a question.

He nodded.

She inhaled slowly, deeply, then took three steps—three *giant* steps—forward, crossing an abyss of twenty-three years.

His arms were ready for her. She stepped into them. She felt the warmth, the lean strength of him, breathed the essence of his strangely familiar scent.

The child who had hidden somewhere inside her all these years relaxed against him, feeling secure once more.

"Father," she whispered. "Daddy."

"Welcome home, daughter," he said. "Tink. Welcome home."

JONAH SPOTTED THE arc of red against the night and followed its path into the dry grass of what constituted the front lawn. He ground out the cigarette until no glow remained, then went up the front porch steps.

Five men were sitting there, telling jokes

and hunting stories and generally having a good time.

"Hey, men," Jonah said casually, "I'd appreciate it if you'd watch the cigarettes. We haven't had any rain since last month, so the grass is dry as tinder."

"Oh, sorry," one of the men said. "That was me. I'm the only one of the bunch who hasn't quit smoking."

"It's tough," Jonah acknowledged. "I read it takes the average person at least five tries before they finally make it. It's supposed to get easier since you know what to expect with each attempt."

"Well, maybe there's hope for me yet."

That launched the hunters on another track—that of sharing their experiences in quitting smoking. Jonah went into the lodge, hung his jacket on the hook behind the door to the office cubicle and began entering the receipts into the accounting program on the computer.

The men's voices were muted now and the place was much too quiet. He glanced at the calendar pinned to the wall above the computer. Monday, October 13.

Well, at least it wasn't Friday the thirteenth.

He finished the task and turned the computer off, then sat there in the three-foot space, reluctant to go into the empty bedroom.

Mary had been over that morning and made dinner rolls and cinnamon buns and a pan of muffins for the guests. Although she'd moved her belongings to the Dalton place, she'd left the stallion here so she could work with him each day when she finished the chores. Then she returned to the other ranch.

Getting up and shoving the office chair out of the way, he went into the bedroom and closed the door. Yawning, he admitted he was tired and should go to bed.

The problem was that there was no sweet slender woman in his bed, waiting to wrap herself around him...

His body reacted predictably at the thought of Mary.

Theresa Dalton, he corrected, although he didn't think of her that way.

Tink.

He liked that better. It's what everyone in the country called her now that her return had made the national news. All the major broad-casting companies had interviewed her and her father and other members of the family for a solid week.

Several filmmakers had wanted to buy the story for a movie, but she'd refused. Seth, the lawyer of the family, had made clear what would happen to any film company who tried to usurp the story and make a movie without Tink's permission.

At the end of the previous week, the news media had cleared out and life had settled back to normal. For the Daltons. For himself, he wasn't sure what normal was anymore.

Recalling the conversation with Aunt Fay while they'd admired the flowers out-side Beau's office, he'd maintained a careful distance from Mary when she faithfully ap-peared, did her work, then left again, as qui-etly efficient as ever.

He brushed his teeth and ignored the taut demands of his body when he crawled be-tween the sheets.

It was a long time before he fell asleep, and morning came much too early. He was to take the men on a trail ride to scout out the best places for the hunt they were planning when deer season opened the following weekend.

THE SCENT OF baking rolls teased his nostrils as he walked down the hallway. Mary was in the kitchen. She smiled at him when he entered. The coffee in the big urn was already perked. He poured a cup.

"How long have you been here?" he asked.

"About fifteen minutes. You slept late."

"Yeah. I couldn't get to sleep last night."

"Is something wrong?"

The worried glance she gave him caused that odd hitch in his chest. He gave a snort of amusement. "Yeah."

She peeked in the oven door, removed the rolls, then tossed the mittens on the counter before studying him.

He knew the moment she realized what the problem was. Her fair skin flushed a becoming pink as she looked away. He sighed loudly. "It's not your problem."

Hiding behind the steam rising from her cup, she murmured, "Maybe it is, or at least it's similar."

He caught the sudden impish gleam in

her beautiful eyes. Now a hot surge of blood joined the uneven beat of his heart. "You're not sleeping, either?"

She shrugged and didn't answer.

Her eyes met his. She didn't have the tinted glasses on this morning. He liked that. The thing he didn't like was the wariness in her gaze. He refrained from following his instincts and crushing her in his arms.

"How's it going over at the Dalton place?" he asked, curious about her life there. The tension that he'd noted in the TV interviews was gone.

"Fine. I'm remembering things—the name of a calf I claimed as a pet, an old hound dog, little things like that. The doll and stroller I got for my third birthday are still there. Aunt Fay put them in my bedroom."

"Is that what you call her? Aunt Fay?"

"Yes. Everyone calls her that, so it seems more natural."

"What do you call Uncle Nick?"

She perused the brightening sky outside the windows for a second before answering. "Father. It was awkward at first, but it's okay now. Everyone calls me Tink. It's both familiar and odd, too. I can't explain…"

He nodded as she stopped speaking. "Breakfast?" he asked.

"That would be great."

He prepared eggs and sausage while she buttered hot biscuits and carried those and their cups into the dining room. There were no sounds from the guests, who'd stayed up and talked into the night.

"It seems like a long time since I've eaten breakfast in here," she said when they were seated.

"Two weeks. A lifetime when you have a new identity, I imagine," he said.

She made a murmur of agreement. "I need to move Attila before it snows. Trevor said if we have a blizzard the roads might be closed for days until the snowplows can get through."

"True, but no storms are predicted. We're having a long Indian summer this year."

He realized she was edgy. So was he. He was trying to be fair, but electricity sizzled whenever they were near each other. It was a strain to keep his distance when he wanted to kiss her senseless each time she appeared.

"I saw your mother in town on Saturday," she said. "I had lunch with her and Trek. People kept interrupting us to say hello and welcome me home."

Jonah recognized the sharp jab, like an elbow in the ribs, as jealousy. "I'm sure there's a line of suitors delighted to welcome you back into the family fold," he said in a wry, teasing tone.

"Hardly." She laughed, surprising him. "Alison's mother has been trying to hook me up with one of the senator's campaign managers. Since she couldn't marry either of her daughters to him, she seems to think I'm a good choice."

"An up-and-coming politician," Jonah remarked as if mulling over the possibility. "He would be a good catch."

She gave him a probing glance, but he ignored the question in her eyes.

"I'd better get to work," she said.

Jonah sat there for a minute after she'd carried her dishes to the kitchen, then left by the back door, letting in a swirl of cold morning air as she did.

He would call his cousin Trek and tell him to back off. Also his mother, who had hinted more than once that the capable wrangler had the makings of a perfect ranch wife.

Mary had a whole world out there to explore, one filled with things she'd never imagined during her days in the orphanage. She needed time and the freedom to discover her role as the daughter of a First Family of Idaho.

She needed to learn she was a very desirable woman and to gain some experience in dating the men who would be attracted, first because of who she was family-wise, then second, because of the person they found when they got to know her—her seriousness and courage and unexpected sense of humor that peeked out like a mischievous imp from those angelic eyes at times.

"Yeah, yeah," he said, glancing over his shoulder as if Aunt Fay were standing there to remind him that Mary needed to be free of complications to find her way in a new life.

He was keeping his distance. He was giving her space. He wasn't using the attraction between them to lure her back into his arms. That was as honorable as he could get.

"And damn difficult," he muttered as he went out to saddle up five horses for the long day ahead.

Chapter Thirteen

Fay Dalton pulled her sweater tightly around her and went out onto the porch spanning the log part of the ranch house. She leaned against her husband. He obligingly slipped an arm around her and shared his warmth.

The middle of October was much cooler than the first of the month had been, although they were still enjoying unusually high day-time temperatures. While a dusting of snow had fallen on the highest peaks, there'd been no snow at all and very little rain so far this season.

Glancing at the tall man she'd fallen in love with as a young woman, she sighed in sat-isfaction. He was her husband now and she was secure in their love. Following his line of sight, she spotted Mary working with a difficult cowpony that Zack had asked her to help train.

The cowgirl guided the horse forward, backward, to one side, then had it wheel in a tight circle.

"She's good, isn't she?" Fay commented.

Nick nodded in supreme satisfaction. "One of the best."

"As she should be, being a Dalton and all." The miracle of finding the child still amazed her. She was glad that her beloved had been reunited with his long-lost daughter, but there was a problem. Every paradise had one. She sighed.

"You're going to have to let her go," she said now.

His head jerked as if pulled by a very inept puppet master. "What are you talking about?"

"Mary. Tink," Fay corrected, using his name for the girl. "She's...lonely."

He snorted as if this was the stupidest thing he'd ever heard. Fay was silent, letting the thought sink in.

As if to enforce the observation, Mary freed the gelding in the pasture and stored the tack in the stable. When she came back outside, she leaned against the fence and stared into the distance like a lost soul yearning for home.

Fay felt the slight tensing in her husband and noted the catch in his breathing while he perused his daughter.

"Did you notice she left her stallion over at Jonah's place?" she asked.

"It's easier for her to work with him over there," Nick said. "Since she insists on continuing her job."

Fay smiled, knowing he didn't like having his child leave his side. He worried about losing her again. In view of their past, the protective attitude was normal. It was also part of the present problem.

The other part, and the part that she feared Nick would have the hardest time accepting, was that his daughter wasn't a child. She wasn't the three-year-old who'd been abducted and was missing for over twenty-three years. She was an adult and a very lovely grown-up woman.

"I think she's in love," Fay murmured.

Not that Tink ever gave a hint of her innermost thoughts or let anyone know if she'd had an unhappy moment since returning to the bosom of her family. She was reticent almost to a fault. And polite. And observant.

The result of being raised in the orphanage, Fay assumed. She had to admit her heartstrings had been tugged as she'd listened to the briefly related facts the girl did disclose about her past. In fact, she'd wept when Nick and his daughter had finally embraced each other and the child had called him "Father" in that shaky, uncertain voice. The entire family had shed a few tears more than once during the following days.

"In love? Who with?" Nick demanded after thinking it over and becoming definitely skeptical about the idea.

"Jonah?" Fay suggested.

"Huh," he said, but he didn't argue about it.

Fay leaned her head against his shoulder and let the idea percolate. Men needed more time than women, in her opinion, to change their perceptions. Or admit they were wrong.

"She probably doesn't know her own mind," he continued after a couple of minutes. "It's only been nineteen days since we learned she was ours. She needs more time to settle in."

"We certainly do, but sometimes…" She let the thought trail off, depending on natural curiosity to cause him to probe further.

"Sometimes what?" he finally asked.

"The heart gets impatient." She paused, then added, "I think she wants to go."

"To Jonah?" he asked in open disbelief.

She refrained from stating it was as obvious as the nose on his face. "Don't you think so? She's so eager when she leaves the house each day to go over and do her work at his place. She's quiet when she returns."

"She's always quiet," he muttered. "Hardest woman to get to talk I ever saw."

Fay didn't smile at his sudden teasing tone. "It's good that she's back with her old family…but it's also time for her to establish her new family. Don't you think so?"

His scowl could have stopped the seven devils of legend in their tracks. For a silent minute, he wrestled with the idea. "Well, I guess. Maybe. Has she said anything?"

"No. That isn't her way. She would suffer

in silence forever rather than do anything to hurt your feelings."

"I think," he finally said, "that you're saying I have to tell her it's okay for her to go back to the other ranch."

"Would it be so terrible if she did? It's just over the next ridge, close enough to visit often."

He looped both arms around her and rested his chin on her head. "You ask a lot of a man. I'm just getting used to being a husband and a father again."

She gave him a fierce squeeze. "You'll still be both. Tink and I share one important trait—we love you and we want to share our lives with you. Even if you are the most stubborn man on the planet."

"Now, Fay, don't go wild in your praise," he cautioned ruefully.

They laughed with the ease of long-time friendship and newly found love. She knew he would do the right thing by his child, just as he had by the six orphans that had been thrust into his care all those years ago, no matter the cost to his own heart.

"I do love you, you know," she whispered.

His arms tightened. "I do know. I love you, too. It's a blessing I never expected at this stage in my life."

Sighing, she let herself relax into him, this strong, honorable man, this man who held her heart so gently...

MARY WAS TIRED, but it was a good kind of fatigue, she mused when she slid into bed that night. The horse Zack had asked her to work with was doing great. He and the twins had been impressed with her training skills.

"A chip off the old block," her cousin had declared after observing the final workout that afternoon when he was finished with his official duties as a lawman.

He and Honey were spending the weekend at the ranch. Roni and Adam were coming up in the morning and would stay over Saturday night. Everyone would be there for Sunday dinner, including Keith, Janis and their toddler.

Everyone except Jonah.

She frowned at the intrusive thought. Jonah was very busy with the guests at the lodge. He'd insisted she take weekends off to be with her new family. In return, she'd left enough prepared food in the refrigerator so that he should be able to get through two or three days without having to do more than heat up stuff.

The hunters, he'd told her, loved the homemade bread, rolls and muffins she'd left for them. Since she enjoyed cooking, especially baking, his words had pleased her very much.

Everything about him pleased her very much, she admitted, forcing her eyelids closed and his image at bay.

Shifting around in the comfortable bed, she tried to force sleep to come. Her eyes popped open. She stared at the ceiling of the pleasant room, which Roni had used as a teenager. The girls would have shared it had she been there to grow up with her cousin.

Mary sighed and turned over on her side. Immediately she recalled how it felt to snuggle spoon-fashion into Jonah's warmth, her cold feet against his legs.

Her eyes snapped open.

Sitting up, she felt around on the floor with her toes until she found her socks. She pulled them on, then went to the window.

The moon had been full a few days ago. Its glow was still bright enough to make out the cattle in the fields. The snow on the highest mountains blended with the clouds surrounding them. Together, they looked like cotton candy, dainty and airy, clinging to the peaks.

The earth no longer shook under her feet when she gazed at the spires of the Seven Devils range. She now understood why her heart had felt impaled on those sharp crags. It had instinctively known this was home and wanted her to know it, too. Now she did.

Her gaze was drawn to the ridge leading to the Devil's Dining Room. Beyond it was the saddle that divided this ranch from the next. From there, one could see the red cliff. A mile from the old ranch house was the lodge.

Where Jonah slept.

Her heart gave a lurch. She sighed as it settled down. She was happy to be here. Really, she was. This was her home. Many things about it felt familiar, and every day she was much more at ease.

Her father had discussed finances with her and her stepmother at Seth's insistence. That had been uncomfortable, as if she was there for the inheritance, but the attorney cousin was very firm about everyone knowing how things stood.

A living trust had been established after Nick's marriage to Aunt Fay—she and the older woman had agreed this form of address seemed the most natural to both of them—now Mary had been added. Trevor and Travis had bought into the ranch operations over the years. Seth had gone over the terms of agreement with the two women. Her father had added his comments and advice during the session in Seth's office.

From orphan to heiress, as one headline had put it. The value of the ranch boggled her mind. Being rich was almost as scary as being kidnapped and abandoned.

Well, maybe not. After all, the consequences were so much nicer. She sighed at the odd thoughts.

Glancing once more toward the north, she paused, then narrowed her eyes as she studied the horizon. There was an odd light in that direction. A reddish glow—

At that moment she heard a telephone ring. Zack's, she thought. As assistant county sheriff, he would be called in an emergency. Her heart squeezed into a ball.

She rushed to the bedroom door and flung it open. A siren sounded in the distance—an alert from the fire tower for the volunteers to answer the summons. She heard feet hit the floor. Zack's door opened and he came into the hall, still fastening his jeans.

"Where is it?" Trevor asked, appearing down the hall, also fastening clothing as he moved.

"The Towbridge ranch," Zack said. He glanced at her. "Jonah's place. Come on if you want a ride."

Mary yanked her boots on and grabbed a warm jacket. Honey and Lyric met her in the living room. She heard her father's voice, then Zack's. Zack reappeared from their end of the house. "Let's go."

Mary and Honey rode with him. Other vehicles fell in line behind them. Zack turned the flashing lights and siren on. They sped off into the night.

A county fire engine turned onto the ranch road ahead of them. Zack followed its trail of dust. When they reached the lodge, a man waved them on toward the back. Mary gasped when she realized the stable and shed were in flames. She heard the angry scream of a stallion.

"Attila," she said. "I asked Jonah to put him in his stall tonight so his leg wouldn't stiffen up in the cold."

Fear formed a gigantic lump in her throat.

"We'll get him," Zack promised, stopping beside the fire truck. They leaped from the SUV and ran forward.

"My horse is in there," she said to the fireman who grabbed her arm as she raced past him.

"You can't go in. The roof is ready to cave." He turned from her and shouted into a bull horn, "Wet the roof of the bunkhouse first. We can't save the stable."

"Where's Jonah?" she asked the fire chief. "Did he move the rest of the horses? Did he get the mules out?"

"Yeah, everything but the stallion. He's in a rage. The two men who went in couldn't get near him."

I can, she wanted to say, but didn't.

When the chief released his hold on her

and moved away, she ran toward the lodge. A wet blanket would protect her and Attila when she led him out. She nearly crashed into a tall form as she dashed up the path lit by flickering firelight.

"Jonah," she gasped. "I need a blanket. I've got to get Attila. He's trapped—"

"I know. I've got a fire blanket."

She saw he held a reflective emergency blanket like those carried by firemen. He also had a wet towel.

"I'll get him," he said, leading the way back to the burning stable at a run.

"No, I'll do it. He trusts me—"

"Here, hold her," he said to someone.

Hands closed on her arms. She struggled as her twin cousins restrained her. "Stay with us," Trevor said.

"Attila is mine," she said fiercely. "Let me go."

"Be still," her father ordered. He and Aunt Fay stepped close and put their arms around her. "Zack knows what to do, what has to be done."

"Zack, wait up," Jonah called out.

Mary looked toward the lawman. He held

a rifle in his hands. It was pointed at the stable. Against the bright aura of flames where some of the wall had already burned away, they could see the dark outline of the big stallion pawing the air as he tried to defend himself from the danger that was closing in all around.

Zack lowered the rifle a fraction. "You can't go in there."

"I have to try," Jonah said.

A crash rent the air as a timber fell somewhere inside.

"No!" Mary cried out. "Jonah, no!"

He glanced her way. His gaze swept over her, gathering her into a visual embrace, then he smiled slightly and dashed through a blizzard of ash and heat and burning embers into the open door of the stable.

Her heart stopped, literally stopped.

The firemen directed two powerful streams of water so that they formed an arc over the man as he leaped over a burning post. The fire blanket covered him, reflecting the flames like a hall of mirrors.

Mary strained against the hands that held her, but she didn't struggle to be free. Neither did she cry out again. Jonah didn't need the added distraction of her voiced fears as he made his way to Attila.

The streams of water swept over the flames above the man and the stallion, dousing the fire where they touched, only to have the blaze rekindle as soon as the stream moved to another fiery section.

Somehow Jonah covered Attila's head with the wet towel. The stallion stuck his nose against the man's back and followed him, hide twitching as embers swirled all around.

Mary held her breath, then let it out in a *whoosh* when both man and horse emerged from the stable. A cheer went up from the crowd.

"Jonah," she whispered hoarsely. She pulled against the hands that held her tightly. "Let me go," she said to her father. "Please."

He glanced at his wife, then released her, holding his hands up so she could see she was free. Mary sprinted across the blackened grass, meeting Jonah and Attila at the edge of the driveway, while the crowd burst into approving laughter.

"I think he's okay," Jonah said, tossing the

towel and the fire blanket aside as Mary came to a halt in front of him. "A few scorched marks—"

He couldn't say another word. Mary flung her arms around him and kissed him as if there was no tomorrow, as if they were alone instead of in the midst of a laughing, cheering bunch of relatives, firemen and strangers.

He wrapped one arm around her, then the other as someone took the stallion and led him away. Nearly three weeks of loneliness vanished in the crush of their lips. When they finally had to come up for air, they stared into each other's eyes.

"Don't you ever scare me like that again," she said in the fiercest tone he'd ever heard.

"No, I won't," he promised. He tried to release her, but his arms just wouldn't give her up.

A crack behind them brought them around to face the last gasp of the inferno. The stable roof collapsed, not with a crash, but with a slow lean toward the paddock. It settled gracefully on the ground with a sound like a tired sigh. The fire hoses pumped water over the dying flames, then on the smoking remains. The fire was out.

More people had arrived during the excitement, Jonah saw. Keith, Janis and the baby. A couple of neighboring ranchers. The senior Daltons. Zack, Trevor, Travis and their wives, were there, too, working with the firefighters to make sure there were no hot spots that could flame once more.

"Well," he said, "shall we go up to the house and put on a pot of coffee?"

Mary moved out of his embrace. She went to the paddock where he'd placed the horses and mules earlier that evening and examined her stallion. Attila nuzzled her hair, which fell around her like a magic veil, as she looked over every inch of his hide, then checked each leg. Jonah waited for her.

When she rejoined him, he looped an arm around her waist and guided her up the path and into the kitchen. There, he found her father and stepmother already had things under control. "Go wash up," Aunt Fay advised both of them.

Without pausing to think, Jonah led Mary to his quarters. He let her use the sink first to wash the soot off her hands and face, to shake the ash out of her hair. He handed her his brush when she stepped back.

He tossed his shirt aside. Mary picked it up and stared at several holes burnt into one sleeve. That arm had been exposed as he led the horse out of the stable. He chuckled when he saw his own blackened face in the mirror. "That's enough to scare babies."

She laughed, a bit shakily but a real laugh.

When he finished, he slipped into a clean shirt. They left their boots in the bedroom and returned to the back of the house. The dining room and kitchen were filled with people, all talking at once, it seemed.

There was a hush when he and Mary reappeared.

"I'd like to thank all of you for your help tonight," he told the volunteers. "Without your prompt actions, we could have lost the lodge, the bunkhouse and the entire crop of winter feed as well as the stable. I'm sure I speak for my partner as well as myself when I tell you we appreciate all you did tonight."

A man stepped forward. He heaved a sigh. "I'm pretty sure it was my fault. I was smoking out by the fence earlier tonight. I thought I ground the butt out when I came in, but I don't know… Maybe it wasn't completely out."

The fire chief got out a pen and spiral notepad. "I have to fill out a report," he said to the man. "Tell me what you remember."

Two hours passed before the discussion was finished and people piled into cars, pickups and fire trucks for the trip home. Most of them were yawning, Jonah noticed.

Finally the hunters went to their rooms. That left four of them in the great room. His glance took in the yawn Mary hid behind her hand and the weariness visible on the faces of her father and stepmother.

"We should go," Aunt Fay said to her husband.

All four stood as if on cue. Jonah saw the older man's eyes go to Mary, then flick to him. He met the level stare and wondered what the other man was thinking. Then they both looked at Mary…Tink.

She glanced at the two men, then moved one step closer to Jonah. "I think I'll stay here. I want to keep an eye on Attila."

Jonah couldn't ignore the leap of his heart at her declaration. He hadn't been sure he could let her go, but he'd thought he would have to.

"That's good," the older woman said, nodding as if they'd all come to the same conclusion. She laid a hand on her husband's arm, giving it a squeeze.

Jonah wondered what message she'd conveyed with that wifely gesture. Emotions, too fast to read, darted through the deep blue gaze, then slowly, almost painfully, the Dalton patriarch nodded.

Mary stepped forward. Father and daughter exchanged hugs. She kissed his cheek. He patted her shoulder. The old man cleared his throat. "Take care of her," he said, then taking his wife's hand, the couple walked out into the night.

"I will, sir," Jonah said. It was a promise.

Mary heard the sound of the engine as her father started the ranch wagon and headed for the Seven Devils homestead. She wasn't sure what to do next, now that she'd made such a fool of herself in front of everyone in that end of the county. She couldn't look at Jonah after throwing herself all over him.

"Mary?" he said. "Tink?"

She loved the husky cadence of his voice. It gave her the courage to meet his eyes. What she saw in those depths was hotter than any fire could ever be. It brought the heat to her face, a sparkling blaze to her heart.

"Yes, Jonah?"

"The devil with going slow and all that," he muttered. "Come here."

He folded her in his arms, gazed into her eyes, then kissed her until she was senseless. Which, she found, was just the way she liked to be kissed.

Eventually they snuggled down on the big, comfortable sofa and kissed some more. A long time.

"Wait a minute," he said, catching her hands as they explored under his shirt. "There's one thing we have to settle." He crooked a finger under her chin so that she had to return his perusal. "Are you going to stay?"

"For how long?" she challenged.

"You know the answer to that," he said, his smile wry. "I want you here forever. You've just found out your real name. Would you be willing to change it again and share mine? Or we can share yours. I'm a modern man, but I have some old-fashioned tastes," he explained. "I want our last name, and that of our children, to be the same."

His smile did things to her heart. "Lanigan is a fine name. I'd like to share it with you."

He rose and helped her up. Arm in arm, they went into the quarters they would share. "We smell like smoke," she told him as they discarded unnecessary clothing.

He shook his head. "You always remind me of the finest perfume—some airy nectar made for a goddess."

They smiled and kissed and nestled under the covers while they made plans for the future because it was their nature to plan and dream.

They agreed on a wedding, to take place very soon. They thought two children sounded just right. A breeding and training school for jumpers was a possibility.

"Or you might want to work with your cousins," Jonah suggested. "You're as skilled as they are."

"Maybe," she said, running her hands down his torso, noticing the flex and strength of his muscles, the long powerful reach of his arms and legs, the solid bone structure beneath that gave form to it all.

"You are so beautiful," she said, wanting much more than words now.

"So are you." He spread her hair over the pillow and gazed his fill of her loveliness. "Did I mention that I love you? I may have forgotten to say it, but I've known it almost from the beginning. I didn't want you to leave."

His words gave her the courage to speak. "I l-love you, too." She paused. "I've never said that to anyone."

He kissed the tip of her nose. "It'll get easier if we both practice saying it every day."

Then they made love, fiercely, tenderly, wildly.

When they settled into sleep, she sighed.

"What?" he asked.

"I used to dream of finding my family and my true self. I thought it would be heaven. And it is." She cupped his face in her palms.

"But it's here, on this side of paradise, that I belong. With you."

He gathered her close. "It's the same for me."

Before the sun came up, they fell asleep, locked in each other's arms.

"Bring in the turkey," Roni directed Adam. Her husband seemed to like her ordering him around. At any rate, he smiled as if he did, and carried a huge turkey to the table in the big dining room. In addition to it and the round table in the kitchen, there was another set up in the living room.

Nicholas Dalton stood out of the way and observed the hive of activity as the family prepared for Thanksgiving dinner, the biggest feast day of the year.

His wife was checking a list to make sure they weren't forgetting anything. Her niece, Lyric, looked over her shoulder. "Yes, we have the gravy. The mashed potatoes are ready," Lyric said, glancing around to check as others stirred, whipped, poured or whatever was necessary to get the food ready.

His gaze went to his daughter, who was sitting on the floor with the toddler, K.J., and the baby, Logan. They were playing with toy cars and trucks that had belonged to the Dalton boys, collected over the course of birthdays and Christmases long ago. Beau's son, Nicky, was building bridges and roads for the cars.

Since both their daughters were present, Fay had suggested they invite the senator—who would begin his duties as the new state governor in January—and his wife to the dinner so they could be with Alison, Janis and their grandson, K.J. Nick had thought that was a good idea. Families should be together at holidays.

Three more babies were expected in the next few months. Roni, Alison and Honey were pregnant. He suspected the other wives would have their own announcements soon, too. The family tree was adding new branches. As it should.

Tink, Roni and the five boys. Seven kids he'd had a hand in raising. Well, he'd had Tink only three and a half years, but she'd grown into a fine woman.

It had been hard to step aside and give her

over to Jonah, but it had been the right thing to do. As his wife had told him. He sighed, a bit sadly, but happily, too, noting the way his future son-in-law gazed at Tink.

"Okay," Fay said, "I think we have everything. Now if we can get this bunch to hush, we can have the blessing before we sit down." She and the women in the kitchen laughed.

It was a sound to warm a man's heart.

His wife came over and put an arm around him. Adam gave a piercing whistle that brought silence to the group. Each husband and wife paired up, holding hands.

Tink came and linked one arm around him, the other around Jonah. His wife and daughter smiled at each other, then looked at him expectantly. Many other eyes, some of Dalton blue, some not, locked on him, all filled with warmth and love.

For a second, his throat closed. He'd lost a beloved wife and a child, but six others had needed him, so life had gone on. Now— he gazed around the room filled with loved ones—to have all this...

He inhaled deeply, then began the blessing that came straight from his heart.

Tink felt Jonah's hand at her waist. He gave her a little squeeze, the silent communication telling her many things—of his love for her, his delight that she'd found her family, his promise that she'd never regret falling in love with him. How could she regret it? He was the most wonderful person she'd ever known. Glancing to her left, she added her father and Aunt Fay to the list. And her cousins and their spouses, and her soon-to-be-family on Jonah's side. His mother and Aunt Fay were engrossed in planning a Christmas wedding for them. She smiled as contentment filled her like a healing balm.

As an orphan, she'd had dreams of finding all this, and so she had. Except reality was so much better than anything she'd dared dream.

Truly, she'd found her bliss.

* * * * *

YES! Please send me the *Cowboy at Heart* collection in Larger Print. This collection begins with 3 FREE books and 2 FREE gifts in the first shipment, and more free gifts will follow! My books will arrive in 8 monthly shipments until I have the entire 51-book *Cowboy at Heart* collection. I will receive 2 or 3 FREE books in each shipment and I will pay just $4.99 U.S./ $5.89 CDN. for each of the other four books in each shipment, plus $2.99 for shipping and handling.* If I decide to keep the entire collection, I'll have paid for only 32 books because 19 books are FREE! I understand that by accepting the 3 free books and gifts places me under no obligation to buy anything. I can always return a shipment and cancel at any time. My free books and gifts are mine to keep no matter what I decide.

256 HCN 0807   456 HCN 0807

Name	(PLEASE PRINT)

Address	Apt. #

City	State/Prov.	Zip/Postal Code

Signature (if under 18, a parent or guardian must sign)

Mail to the Harlequin® Reader Service:

IN U.S.A.: P.O. Box 1867, Buffalo, NY 14240-1867
IN CANADA: P.O. Box 609, Fort Erie, Ontario L2A 5X3

CAHBPA13B

ReaderService.com

Manage your account online!

- Review your order history
- Manage your payments
- Update your address

> *We've designed
> the Harlequin® Reader Service
> website just for you.*

Enjoy all the features!

- Reader excerpts from any series
- Respond to mailings and special monthly offers
- Discover new series available to you
- Browse the Bonus Bucks catalog
- Share your feedback

Visit us at:

ReaderService.com

REQUEST YOUR FREE BOOKS!
2 FREE NOVELS PLUS 2 FREE GIFTS!